I0703537

# 

***The Troyuan Chronicles, Book 9***

by Ernest Velon

book reviewed by Nicole Yucaba

*"He inhaled everything quickly going back for seconds and thirds. The only dish he refused was a cooked Venusian Rat."*

Beginning with the inquisition of Alack by the Inquisitor Themis Magistrate, readers enter a fantastical realm where friends in high places mean protection for those who oppress the masses. At the heart of a dispute are internal governmental and galactic struggles which test the characters, and particularly Alack, in moral and ethical ways. Alack's adventures continue, and the plot follows him as he encounters strange rituals in which he is the guest of honor, breaks taboos, and comes across history and beings as ancient as the universe itself. As the book concludes, readers once again find the protagonist in a struggle for survival against an unimaginable monster with the power to potentially destroy everything.

With its subtle critiques of high government and government officials, this novel reads like a sci-fi allegory for contemporary times. Even Alack's cultural clashes, particularly at the scene regarding Mrs. Walliskon's cremation, wax reminiscent of modern societies navigating an ever-interconnected globe where cultural taboos and expectations may shock others. The protagonist is a memorable and often humorous character whose eccentricities, like his swift overeating, make readers laugh out loud. Alack's adventures with other beings and their wartorn history might also remind readers of current discussions regarding efforts to understand and decolonize history. Thus, once again, the book transforms from a mere sci-fi novel to a book with a larger commentary on the way civilizations have functioned for centuries.

Both sci-fi and mystery fans will enjoy this novel because it is a fusion of both genres. Readers looking for a new, humorous hero will appreciate Alack for his all-too-human vulnerabilities and faults (like his inability to submit a properly proofread report to his superior), which easily make him the book's most memorable character.

# TROYUAN CHRONICLES

## BOOK NINE

by

Ernest Velon

**Gotham Books**

30 N Gould St.
Ste. 20820, Sheridan, WY 82801
https://gothambooksinc.com/

Phone: 1 (307) 464-7800



Registration Number: TXu 2-363-306
Effective Date of Registration: March 03, 2023
Registration Decision Date: April 06, 2023

Published by Gotham Books (June 23, 2023)

ISBN: 978-1-956349-37-5 (H)
ISBN: 979-8-88775-229-7 (P)
ISBN: 978-1-956349-36-8 (E)

# OTHER BOOKS BY THIS AUTHOR

- The Man from Hardin
- Troyuan Chronicles Book One
- Troyuan Chronicles Book Two
- Troyuan Chronicles Book Three
- Troyuan Chronicles Book Four
- Troyuan Chronicles Book Five
- Troyuan Chronicles Book Six
- Troyuan Chronicles Book Seven
- Troyuan Chronicles Book Eight
- Thracian Eferratus

# TABLE OF CONTENTS

# FOREWORD

The wife and I decided on an ambitious expedition to locate the 'Valley of the Emperors', some where's outside the ancient Capital Area. According to lost legends and folklore history, this area, a flat plain stretching several Sectals into marshy swamp lands, was the sight of monumental buildings and pleasure palaces by the later Emperor Akopion in 3035 UT. A colossal maze of spectacular architecture sprawled out amongst  courtyards, forms, gardens, and huge pleasure pavilions. According to our piecing together of legends and tales, this was a secluded place for the weary and the overworked potentates of the Amazian Empire, called the Mendozian. It was a place where the Emperors could entertain without the public's eye upon the Amazitine, the Mastatine and Castravine hills. So, gathering a few field hands from the locals, we set off.

Our local guides told us a colony of Fribonites occupied the area next to where the Valley was supposed to be. They advised us that these small, hairy creatures were excellent workers who would assist us in the digs. So, I purchased many tools to assist them in their work. We were told they are primitive and do not have our type of instruments. Their planet Largos suffered an ecological disaster, and these were the survivors, who relocated here to Amazia. Arriving at the colony, we were received with great ceremony and feasting. Our interpreter explained our mission and asked for their help in digging away the topsoil. They agreed, and we gave them the tools.

But before we can begin the work, we must find the Valley.

Ascending in a hot air balloon, we could see the bumps and

ripples of buried foundations not too far off. The use of the balloon was the only means of Arial flight we had to do this. During these far lost future times, we have gone back than forward, a sad state of our ancient ancestors would find appalling.

Marking out certain places to begin we studied the crabgrass and small mounds of dust weed around. Sometimes in the 6000's UT, these buildings and pavilions were abandoned and plundered for their rare and costly materials. Travelers report afterwards even the inner cement and steel infrastructure was removed and sold. The drainage system became clogged and slowly the Valley returned to its original swampy, marshy appearance. What we expected to find when we started digging is unknown, since everything had been stolen away.

Returning to the Fribonite colony with our sight plans, we found the funny little black and hairy people wearing our tools. I realized they had no conception of what they were for except of body ornamentation. We had to show them in a physical manner how to use these implements that we humanoids developed. Once this done we marched to our marked sight and began going down to the foundations. Finding floors of beautiful tiles and marbles, of designs never seen since three thousand years, made our hearts stop in awe. We had discovered the lost legends of the Mendozian sagas. In one exposed chamber, under layers of debris, we found the 'eye in the reeve' symbol. This reminded us of the exploits of Alack Troyus, who might have wandered these halls so long ago. With that inspiring our thoughts we continued to reveal the lost past.

Ernest Velon

Larentia, 07/15/9841 U.T.

2

# THE VATADOS AFFAIR

By Ernest Velon


"You claim sovereign rights over the accused?" shouted the Inquisitor Themis Magistrate down from his high bench. "You claim a specialism that supersedes the common law of the land. You thwart the mechanizations of our local police in pursuit of your ambitions. You have trampled the lawful rights of patriotic citizens of this planetary realm, and you have disregarded the sacred oaths of those whom you imprisoned as false, all to uphold the Code of Dwitinton." An ugly frown washed over the plastic whitewashed face under the silly frock hat. "You stand accused of violations without limits against the Supreme Royalty and his Magnita of friends and relatives. Before we condemn you may speak in your defense, Colonel Troyus."

Alack, who refused to kneel, stood defiant before the Themis, the High Arch Inquisitor of Alpha Vatados. His blood still boiled-with legal anxiety over the intrigues and shenanigans from the Telefonia Affair, making his fortitude strong like a Seminian mountain. Chained by the local Ravashor (constable), Alack felt the iron links dig into the torn, dirty white fabric of his polo shirt. They had padlocked his muscular arms with extra shackles after he took down a dozen of their Palasatro Guards in a street fight. Around his powerful thighs and upper leg muscles, more crisscrossing heavy metal links ripped into his black pants, preventing further assaults of his lethal martial arts moves. His assignment called for the apprehending of a political runaway from Imperial Justice, but nothing like this.

With friends in high places, they protected their own kind from the Special Service Agent even to the point of false arrest. Trumped up charges and paid witnesses caused his efforts to be halted on the very threshold of achievement. He captured his criminal and brought him before a lesser judge for sentencing. But the magistrate had Alack wait outside of the courtroom as the Judge allowed the Criminal to escape by the back door. Taking the law into his own hands, he caught the fleeing man, but others interfered. A full knockdown brawl on the city streets plastered police and people as Alack went ballistic in anger. Now he boldly faced this high civic Official who represented the family of nobles who protect their own kind. Tired and hungry, Alack decided on a rash, bold move of Seminian raw defiance.

"The advantage always is with people on the inside." Alack inhaled, making a necessary decision. He could easily break these chains and shackles. He has done it before, tossing the flying pieces in their faces, but decided not too. This world has no SSG and Praetorium he can fall back upon for help. What he painfully discovered in the street brawl he is quite alone here. Better to bow to their way, not the arrogant Seminian way. "You're Honor, may it please your bench to remove these bonds, it will make my defense less painful and add greater dignity to your court."

The pastel whitewashed face glared down, made a gesture, and they took away his shackles. "You are on your good behavior, Colonel."

"I can't talk with all that stuff around my body, that's much better." Alack saw how shocked they are. He is free and stepped up to the high altar of Justice. "Your Honor, those accusations are false and the evidence is lies and clever deceit. Yes, I uphold the Imperial Code, and that body of spatial law gives me the power to hunt down and bring to justice the accused. If I may have been too forceful in my endeavors then, it's because the accused used his influence to block and stymie my progress. If I seemed indifferent to your unwritten laws and customs, it's because I am in earnest to achieve my goals. I ask you to consider my plight and withhold your judgment."

A twisting smirk broke the caulked covered face. "What counter evidence do you present that will sway my wrath?"

"One, I am an officer of the Emperor of Amazia. We may wear different clothes, but you and your court and I have the same purpose." Alack used his long dirty fingers numbering off the mental items. "Two, the accused, Azar Massar while under oath has slandered many Amazian politicians and businessmen of good standing, while taking bribes from opposing parties to perform such nefarious services. Three, Massar has published false articles and ugly news bulletins that caused terrible damage and influenced the honesty of the voting public. Four, Massar has defiled and abandoned several young females of their virginity stealing their wealth, abandoning fatherless siblings and violated their religious rights. Five, he has used his influence to fill public authorities with his friends, family and relatives, utterly ignoring qualification laws and terminating the more skilled and experienced workers, and six, I quote Seminia's greatest legal mind, Bala Ropa, 'without approval of power, of success in justice and wisdom, public representatives can not gain a proper and great noble character'."

"That particular witticism has no grounds in this court."

Alack frowned then blew air from his cheeks, deriving another tactic. "I quote Amazia's greatest legal mind, Civius Proctor, 'you must earn your trust. It can not be bought or legislated by those of good or bad intentions.'"

A caustic nod of futility from the white washed frown, "and that plays no part before my court."

Alack did a funny half walk and turn, "Alright, I'll play on your Fix Ball court. I quote Ambashkon, Unapiteria's greatest legal philosopher 'higher levels of civilization also mean greater levels of treachery'."

"He also spoke 'two plus two can equal five'. Ambashkon was also a great scholar of antiquity and riddles. Since you like quotes, I'll entertain one. A young lad climbed a Baramoore tree to gather its tasty nuts, but he tried all day but came home with none, why?"

Alack knew this one, it's as old as ancient Norume on Amazia. Putting on a thinking scowl, finally replied. "You say why, Sir? Because the Baramoore tree does not produce eatable nuts, the Sayamoore tree does."

The Judge blew air from his plastered cheeks in frustration, "Azar Massar is a friend and consular of the Inamoratas Queen and a stout supporter of the Shuton Magnita on Vatados. As such, your evidence was confiscated as per the suppressing of information of defamation." A long, arrogant sigh issued from the pastel lips. "Such false material cannot be used in my court, Colonel."

"But your Honor, that evidence is not false beyond the skies of this planet. I would not have journeyed twenty-eight light years, plus many diversions, to hunt down my prey."

"Azar Massar is a man, not an animal, Colonel."

"He is a fugitive from Amazian justice and will be treated as such by me until he is caught, tried, and judged.  Accept no task unless you are equal to its burdens.  I have Consular Imperium."

"Not on this planet.  He has rights on our soil, Colonel, not to be trampled by your Code or self-proclaimed arrogance."

"When dealing with spatial criminals, the Code of Dwitinton goes beyond all planetary laws, Sir.  It is the glue that binds the Imperium together."

"We on Vatados think differently.  Your Code applies to trade, immigration, banking, and other technology, not civil rights.  Azar Massar is a prominent citizen of great worth to the Shuton Inamoratos. He is SC, Shuton's Council, and above such falseness.  Also, as such, what I witnessed with our restraints, tells me you must leave our world." Not allowing Alack to speak further, he slipped on a gruesome metallic black glove and slammed his palm on a thick block of white stone.  "I sentence you to incarceration until an SSG Representative arrives and takes you off world for punishment on your own soil.  Case closed!"

"My proceedings, you watched–them or not?" asked the Judge frowning while washing off the white facial makeup.

"Why should I?  I know you'll do a thorough job ridding our planet of him."

"I had to debase that unsavory ant, Azar," spoke Masa Avallania, the Themis (high judge) of Hunterdome County and the capital city of Waltsba.  "We can't have Amazians fighting in our streets, subverting our laws, and tarnishing our cherished ways.  We are the 'old stock', the

Magnita, and death takes us unto the end of our days. May the ancient Shutons rule Vatados forever." Masa Avallania smiled at his guest as the tall, skinny fellow in the long maroon tunic and cape returned the smile. A delightful air of calm settled in his office in the citadel of Waltsba. "We've had others come here to upset the status quo but the secret Laws protect us and give me the power to act unrestrained, unto a death is necessitated. That ant had the answer to my riddle, what is the cosmos coming to?" A long-finalized sigh closed the topic. "Where are you off to now?"

"Not a bad one, Masa, I'll use it to confound the idiots at my ball." Azar Massar swished his cape around the room in a happy exuberance motion. "Too my southern plantation and property, I've been away so long I've forgotten what the sweet Turnolves smell like and the gratifying noise of a whip on Noxi bare flesh." He gave his friend a sideward's glance, "I had it good on Amazia. I made a lot of credits, more than you can count in a lifetime. Whatever I said went. People believed the rubbish and slander I poured into their minds."

"My father said if a lie is fantastic enough, people will believe it."

"And they certainly did. My credibility was so good I just had to frown at a politician, and that made stellar headlines. Damn…I was good." He chuckled. "I made and broke them at a whims fart. They called me Star Maker or Breaker. Their wives, the ones who loved the husband's wealth more than the man, came crawling to me begging to stop the slander. What they gave me, how far they were willing, all decided if I will trash the fool or not. They stumbled over another to please me, one little mistake, one false innuendo, and a career went sliding into the dumpster." He laughed. "But all good things come to an end. I won't miss it, only the credits I have to show." He burst out in sadistic laughter. "Did you know I almost started a stellar war with my brand of yellow slander? We had arms dealers, all sorts of businessmen, and even a few bureaucrats ready to move, what a shame, it would've been so exciting and glorious!"

"I heard tales over an inquiry by the local Senators and others, true?"

"Yes, but don't believe their data, only my lies." A long pause followed then a confident finger was whipped out from the engulfing cape. "Only one I couldn't fool. That SSG Insect whose evidence overturned a decade's work of mayhem and false reporting. He saw right through me, as clear as that nose on your face, Masa. He brought me down, made me squirm, and crawl away to your arms. Just make sure that SSG Asshole never comes back to haunt me."

"Fear least the God's wrath, if more of his kind do come..." giggled the Themis, "I'll invoke the Nosh Vis'blk, our secret legal language, by our law we can use it for legal protection, and I know, their ear translators don't contain the digital codex. What the ear will hear is not what we say. I have used that spoken word to get a self-incriminating verdict quite often." His whiny giggle turned into a nasty gurgling chuckle. "We are still an independent world with a unique charter that can never be revoked."

"That'll stick in his ass. See you at the Shuton's Balaska Ball."

"Certainly..."

And Azar Massar, in one mighty bellow of the fancy cape, is gone.

The Toshivic Revolution exploded on Amazia in 1731 UT. At first, it was localized to a few malcontents in the suburbs of a few major cities. The Unapiterians, after two hundred years of unbridled luxury and exploitation, only considered it a policing action by the Palasatro Guards. The few families that controlled ninety percent of the wealth of the galaxy were too entrenched in their own selfish, meager priorities to pay attention to the fires starting way down below. The Amazians, united under Elvir DeGram, a sub-Shuton who survived the 'reign of poison' under Shuton Kalcon, had neither a good general or an inspiring leader, but he who was a fine clerk and a brilliant organizer. He created the Grand Regency, marshalling the ancestral leaders of the old Pre-Evil nations. At first, ancient chemical weapons were used, long since stockpiled by the nations for such a day. Attacking at night, stealing the more modern weapons, the revolt grew and expanded. By the time the Unapiterians realized they had a serious problem sent Waverin-Mass (armed troops), but it was too late. The Amazians were winning driving the oppressors off world.

After the Amazians won the Toshivic Revolution and kicked away the tyranny of Unapiter in 1831 UT, many Star Masters used this opportunity to seek a better career. Starved from promotions by the Magnita nobles, they sought desperate means to advance themselves. As the Treaty of DeGram was being negotiated by the new Amazian Corostat planetary council, led by Star Master Balaska, a local governor over fifteen thousand solar systems in the Jovia-Oronis (Orion Spur) Quadrant suddenly defected to the Amazians. He established a spiraling precedent for other Star Masters as they fragmented the Unapiterian Celestial Empire throughout the Fylight (Milky Way) galaxy. After all the seething dust had settled, Unapiteria was a mere speck of its former glory. Large swaths of stellar territory, captured by the Unapiterian star lords in the middle 1550's UT, had jockeyed for prestige and power, with most joining the fledgling Amazian nation to get a better piece of the galactic pie.

"This planet is…uh…how would you say, different?" Began Special Counsel to the Amazian Ambassador's office of Alpha Vatados, "They have Eminent Charter, approved by Emperor Hindonborg early in his administration, over two hundred years ago, part of the Star Master Balaska Accords, which ceded this portion of Byloria Regent too the Amazian Imperium, and over nine thousand major Class A planets of considerable wealth were part of the deal, but this here one is special, Colonel."

"How special is special? Where's the Praetorium?" Alack had finished inhaling his prison meal and looked around for another helping. "I've got to get more to eat!"

"Nothing of the sort, Colonel. No Ackard Police or SSG interference, the Palasatro have total autonomy except in high military matters, and a pittance of revenue for the Amazian coffers, versus the standard thirty percent. An off-world business or of any such merchants or industry cannot take up house here without serious investigation and scrutiny. Even if approved, all workers must be of the local population, except for a single stellar representative."

"Thanks!" mumbled Alack as the funny little Amazian placed another dish on his cell's table. "No Curlator? No SSG, No Code…nothing? This isn't the simple legal Telefona Affair…I thought I can breeze through this."

"It's like we've gone back to the Pre-Evil times, the Shutons of old Unapiter still hold sway here, and chew your meal slowly, I don't think I can get a third helping."

"This was never in my briefing…I'll strangle my Boss!" Alack licked the shiny plate clean. "I live to eat…but…?" A questioning frown brought his head up making eye contact. "What is this stuff…its awful?"

"The local prison gruel. They feed it to the slave labor in the southern latitudes..."

"Slave labor!"

"You're not the only one who stumbled upon this place, Colonel Troyus. We've been trying to force them to end that horrible evil for decades. But they hide behind their Eminent Domain Charter and payoff any Senitiumor who wants to change it in the Senitium. Even Aqualayon and his pro-civic party have been stymied at every turn."

"If this was an AOP world, I would expect these terrible conditions to exist, but it's not." Alack exhaled, long and frustrated, "treacherous weapons don't make brave men."

"Time stands still here."

"But Azar Massar is not a temporal mistake, but a social one. He has ruined many honest men in government with lies and false news reporting, he's managed to slip through my fingers because he has wealthy backers," Alack stood up. "All the good hardworking people with honest intentions he destroyed, and I MUST GET HIM!"

"I know how dedicated you are Colonel. I sympathize with you, really I do. My own uncle was wrecked by his creative slander, but here I'm helpless. All the ancestors of the exiled Shutons, those who fled after the fall of Celestial King Artolos in 1831, still hold a terrible grip on reality."

Alack's long, dirty fingers pressing on his abdomen as it began to make loud gastric noises. "That shit had no effect. You must get me out of here before I shrivel up and go puff!"

"My embassy has been given the authority to do just that. But you must sign these extradition papers saying you'll never come here again or be seen on Alpha Vatados soil." He held out the legal Calcomp.

Alack made a flash decision, placing his sense of duty over his signed word.

Okay, Colonel, you're free…to follow me to the Amazian embassy, and home."

Shaking himself in the torn polo shirt, Alack inhaled, stretching and almost tearing the fabric under his arms and shoulders, then calmed down. "Does your embassy have a kitchen?"

"If we leave now, the cook will be starting his cuisine talents."

Alack never stopped eating.

He inhaled all they gave him, and gulped down every scrap of leftovers they had in the icebox. Still not satisfied, his black hole belly went after the snack food machine and a box of granola bars a secretary was selling as a fund raiser. But what finally fulfilled his wild metabolic rate was a street vendor called the 'roach coach' who stopped on the embassy grounds during lunch time. In a mad frenzy to top off a sickening desire to eat everything, Alack cleaned the fellow out. They found him resting on a bench in the backyard under the sheltering leaves of a large fern tree with bright yellow flowers.

Stretched out on the wooden stone bench, Alack held his belly, the abdomen muscle striations flattened into a painful bonded steel bulge, the torn polo shirt ripped and hanging from his utility belt. On his handsome face a delighted expression of bliss. So stuffed he is breathing from his upper diaphragm until his crazy hyper metabolic rate burns off enough calories so he can move.

"You're like a Brenzini lizard," began the Ambassador disgusted, "they lay around for hours in the sun to warm up. You're a bigger pig than what I heard about you Colonel."

"King of pigs…if it's good enough for the septic system, it's for me!" Alack finally stirred. He shot up like a bolt of charged lightning. "You try living off that gruel with a furnace for a body…" Taking a deep breath, Alack stretched, grasping at the air above his flock of auburn hair. They witnessed a remarkable sight of raw Seminian ribs and pectorals popping and straining. A dangerous redness creased the color of his tan flesh as the upper body mass increased by a third of its size.

"So…that's how you broke their chains…"

"Strength makes all values possible." The raw mass of muscles and groaning sinew dropped down to its ripped normal appearance. "I hate any type of restraints." Alack stood and shucked his excellent built torso like a canine shaking off water. A warm smile broke his heavy lips as those intense brown eyes looked at the Ambassador and his aides. "Sorry about all that eating, but I was starving and very depressed. When I hit rock bottom, I just want to bury my face in a mountain of eats." More inhaling and exhaling, "if I caused any embarrassment or damage, I'll pay what I ate or broke." He flashed them a quick smile with the ends of his lips drawn up. "Just let me clean myself and get some new clothes, and I'll be on my way."

"Of course, Colonel, we have your valise and Calcomp. A squad of Palasatro Guards awaits outside–to escort you off Vatados…when you're ready."

"Don't hesitate to vegetate…" he muttered.

Donning a new set of leisure field clothes, Alack is escorted to the Space and Jet port of Vatados. They made sure he boarded the PULTA space liner, and once it blasted off climbing rapidly into the crystal bluish red skies of the planet, they left feeling another irritating Amazian is off their soil. But what they did not see was the maintenance worker, with his toolbox and digital analyzer strung over a broad shoulder, securing the lower cargo hatch as the pilot did his final flight liftoff check. The Worker wore a floppy hat to protect his long hair from grease and bio-hazardous particles, a covering jumpsuit and hanging utility belt, passed without notice through the cordon of gold and red uniformed Palasatro policemen.

Once alone in a secluded area near the anabolic digesters and low priority storage area of the port, Alack removed the dirty coveralls and silly hat. He dressed in the long blue pantaloons with cream colored puffy shirt the locals wear. On his snug utility belt, he hung various carrying pouches, his valise he changed the exterior fabric color to a pleated pattern resembling the traveler's carpetbag. Checking his false ID he stole from the Embassy, this will get him by if he is stopped by the Palasatro. Feeling satisfied, Alack took a running leap and dashed over the wire sensor net fence.

In this Affair he is on his own.

There is no SSG or Special Service office he can fall back upon for help. There is no Special Customer Service department (the SCS) to create a false bio or make a covert identity. There is no Placement Bureau (the PB) where he can fit into a world's social structure or be tailored for a false corporate entity. There is no Department of Eyes (Cosmic Surveillance) that provides all Agents with detailed information on the world and social habits an Agent will operate in. No Elanus to come running to save his star agent from certain death. Nothing. Knowing this, Alack took a walk to a small suburban library where he did his own research and put together a false identity to suit his physical characteristics. The people of Alpha Vatados are from the same racial stock of the Amazians, the Trijan- Calistus-Canopus Clan (Triple C races of the Orion Spur). There are a few large humanoids in the mountainous regions up north that fit his Seminian size and looks.

Satisfied, found a mass transit bus stop and waited for public transport to leave the environs of the capital city Waltsba. He had stolen enough Jupents from the snack machines, the local currency, to get him into the rural interior, down south. It is somewhere there that Azar Massar has a country hideaway.

The funny old lady at the crude, but quaint 'Inn at the Cross' stared at the long-haired dirty traveler in the torn frock coat, baggy mud-stained pants, boots with holes, and a foul-smelling carpetbag on a pole. Her eyes are used to the clothing from many others but her intuitive feelings after catching the boyishly handsome face, big brown eyes, heavy lips, and high cheeks, told her differently. In that handsome face a deep desire moved. Something her late husband never left her, the inner need, the natural yarning, what a mother's heart always wanted? Seeing the beautiful flock of dirty auburn hair knew this is the son she craved.

"Do come in Youngman, we have a small…" the tramp Traveler is far taller than she thought, "a large room to rest your weary hide, "The overwhelming odor of cooking stew and baked bread made the youthful face swoon. A stumbling weakness passed between the unsteady legs as she led him to a chair next to a big wooden butcher-block table. "Why don't you sit and enjoy a moment of my cooking." With a terrible gusto the unkempt Stranger inhaled everything she had, even the stale leftovers from the previous day, while licking the pots and pans she just used but have not cleaned as of yet. "My, by the great fanged owl, you were wrought of a belly stuffing?"

After a loud pleasing burp, the young Stranger came alive. "I thank you from my bottom all the way up…thanks!" He leaned back in the chair content. "I've been eating the roads dust since yesterday…no meals…nothing but watermelons and Tacards (apples) I stole from nearby trees…I have no money but I'm willing to work…you say a room awaits?"

The elderly Lady smiled. Her wrinkled face and haggard nose and cheeks lit up like a sunrise. "Oh yes, if you're willing to stay and help me. My husband died in a duel and left me this Inn to tend to. I'm good at cooking, the beds, laundry, the clients, but timber repairs, I'm not."

"I am, fair Lady, I am. I come from the north seeking better places in the southern regions for my living. I shall dwell her amongst your generosity until it no longer haunts your fair and honest limbs. Life is a choice."

"Oh…such flowers in your tongue are not needed here, Youngman. What comes through that front porch door is fit for a crude meal, a dirty bed, and a few stolen Jupents for my coffers. So, beware, suspicions ghost you might enliven and that may cause problems."

"The journey brings us happiness, not the destination." Alack gently pulled on his ear, adjusting the language translator to a lower setting. His act seemed as if he was in deep quick insight. "I thought being so near the plantation estates, you're cliental would be on a higher rung on the social ladder."

"You flatter my humble self, Youngman, but they of the land royalty harkens to the modern hotels in glass and steel that touch the clouds. Only stable masters and the brown collar workers come here, and maybe a runaway seeking freedom?"

"Then you help slaves who-have escaped?"

"What more can be said. The Palasatro gets'em before the sun sets, there is no hope for the poor in debt."

"I have heard the poor in debt sell themselves to the taskmaster because their plight is of their own doing. A gambling, whoring, seeking more than what's satisfying in the home with a devoted wife and lovely children, they lay it upon themselves. Fortune is the most unstable of all things under the sun."

"Such banter is only a surface. Seek what is beneath, and there's more to their story. A restless man may come and go looking beyond their homely life, but life teaches a hard lesson if one allows the eye and mind to wander." She poured him a glass of some sweet lemon drink. "Your room is in the barn east." Alack finished the drink, and both stood. "It belonged to one as you but escaped from a missing maiden he owes much to. Runaways are not all of the bondage sort."

She took Alack out back to a sturdy two story barn, up a side of wooden stairs to a large, well-kept apartment big enough for his size. "This I like!" He dropped his pole and bag on the floor, bounced on the bed, touched everything, opening dresser drawers, and examined the toilet facilities. A large barrel with a water spigot hung from the ceiling. "You have running water?"

"Only when it rains. A water collector on the main roof catches the tears from the clouds. It is full now from weekly showers. He who was here last installed a fine system." She opened a closet full of musty clothes. "It's an accumulation of sorts from those who stayed a little but ran when the heat or the rent came. Some may fit you."

"Then I shall partake, rest, and join you in two hours, good Lady."

"I am Matilda of the Inn at the Cross, yours?"

"The name given at birth is Alack of the Iron Fist." He yanked up his ripped sleeve and popped a massive bicep of veins and hardened sinew. "I have come down from the northern hills to taste the southern haunts, and as far as I see, I like."

"Ha! Wisely chosen!" and she left humming a tune.


The next day Alack is up early, he had a chance to check the Inn out yesterday and its adjacent buildings. He already saw several jobs of simple carpentry and made a mental list. As he worked, replacing planks and hammering down popped nails, memories flooded in about his early days at Villa Hardin. The skills he learned as a ground's keeper for

Elanus returned, making his jobs easier. Only one problem, this planet has not kept up with the advances in technology as has Amazia, and he had to find ways of doing repair work without the modern tools. But the challenge is there, and Alack enjoys a good challenge to make his brain work and sharpen his skills. By noon, he is ravenous and sought Matilda's kitchen.

She caught his sweet body odor and beheld a behemoth in black shorts, dirty work socks, and boots. Beautiful muscular legs building up to a powerful torso, slim waistline, a barrel chest with massive trapezoids, broad and expansive shoulders holding powerful arms with ripped biceps, and topping it all off with a flock of long, bouncy auburn hair curling down to the thick neck and shoulders. The face, a bright burst of youthful big brown eyes, high cheeks, thick lips, the whole affair between the softness of a boy and the hardening features of a man, stood before her demanding food, and lots of it.

Matilda fed him.

As Alack numerated on his long fingers all the work he did since the morning she served dish after dish until he is satisfied. With each job completed another pewter plate is slowly dropped before him, one on top another, making a small high-rise. As he swallowed in one titanic gulp a whole pitcher of lemon juice, she asked a curious thought. "The Ravashor and his party will be here on the morrow, maybe a hiding you should take?"

"What's a Ravashor?" followed by a pleasing burp.

"The local traveling Palasatro and his hordes, who collect taxes, put to trial the criminal, gather the condemned, catch runaways and abuse the women folk for pleasure and favors. This Ravashor is not as bad as last one. A restraining took place two years ago by the plantation gentry, seems foul play was caught, and a slacking and sacking of the former took place."

"When the light goes away, the darkness comes to play. Why are you telling me this, good Woman?" Alack sucked in a massive amount of air, gave a sinew life stretching of tensile muscle and limbs, then exhaling to his fine ripped norms.

"If he has a picture from his previous, he maybe recognizing?"

Alack thought about this one. If this was a regular world of the Imperium with SSG and Praetorium, yes, the traveling Prefect, who reads the Service Bulletins, would know his pretty features. But here, on Alpha Vatados, as far as he can see, there has been no effort at surveillance technology for criminality, or a truly modern police organization. Maybe in the major cities but out in the rural farming areas, very primitive standards apply. He broke a fine smile showing all whites. "I assure you, fine and cautious Lady, what I ran away from she who is not to be named, has not made me a poster face on the Palasatro's latrine or in their brothels. I have no bad records to speak of, only a strong will to escape the dungeon of a marital mistake, which you so wisely know about from others."

"Are there be children in this mistake?"

"No, just many greedy relatives and a powerful manipulative mother with a whip in one hand and a tongue that's sharp as a sword, in the other."

Matilda's creaky old face stretched in a delightful grin. "Ha, such stories I have heard, and what you seek is rejuvenation. You will find it here, Alack of the Iron Fist Matriarch."

"That's well said.  I shall be your waiter when the Ravashor and his men arrive."

"But be warned, do so in humble ways and not be seen much."

They poured into the Inn the next day.

Thirty rugged looking men of large hefty size dressed in tunic like jackets of rustic leathers and sack cloth pants. They were all armed with sword, knife, whip, truncheon and ten others holding spears. Conical hats with the ancient Unapiterian symbol with cross lines dividing and the end ovals.  Only the Ravashor is armed with a photonic blaster, but it has rusted stains and a crimson streak of red where the ray cell normally is.  This told Alack it is only for show; the ray cell malfunctioned and burned away the capacitors in the firing chamber long ago.  Dragging a dozen ragged men in chains the traveling Palasatro Guards tied them to the posts on the porch in a resting sitting position so they can use their hands for drinking.

"Where's that fine hospitality, Matilda!  We are hungry and thirsty!" Shouted the tall lean Ravashor Karta in a red and gold traveling uniform, "if my herald did his job a hearty welcome we expect!" Matilda came from the kitchen with Alack in tow.  She has a new apron on and cleaned herself looking very ladylike as a proper hostess.  "Ha! With such as this my wife will get jealous…" he grabbed her giving the happy wrinkled face a kiss and hug.  His delighted black eye saw Alack and went serious.  "Who be this mountainous Stewart bumpkin?"

"Serve our good guests."  Obeying, Alack dressed in brown boots, black shorts, his utility belt snuggly around a slim waistline, a tight white sleeveless shirt with collar, and his hair meticulous styled, bounced as he passed out drinking goblets to the men.  "I just hired him for your arrival, pleased?"

"Yes, you've done well…" gently releasing her, the hard face with mustache, and eye patch studied the big muscular young man, who pulled out chairs and guided the Palasatro Guards to tables filling up the room. "Boy…step here!" In a quick servant manner, Alack stood before him looking down. "Where do you hail from? You're not the normal shit stock of the locals."

"I'm from the Northern Mountain province of Masalotus, village of the Twin Falls."

"Name? They gave you one, I should hope?" His good eye is all over the stout chest stretching the shirt's fabric. Karta started to walk around Alack studying the legs, the back, expanded sides, and very broad shoulders.

"Alack of the Iron Fist Clan."

"I am pleased at what I see…" The Ravashor pounded Alack's cement like shoulder with a sturdy fist. "Look at this!" All his men stopped drinking and focused their attention upon Alack. "I am proud to be of the Unapiterian race knowing this is what is growing and coming down from the highlands these days. Be proud and happy!" Matilda pushed a fancy goblet into his hand. "I drink to the Iron Fist family from faraway Twin Falls. Long live the Shuton!" Repeating, they all drank. "Ha…you can resume your duties, Alack of the Iron Fist. Our stomach's concern is now with the good Lady of the Inn at the Cross."

Alack served them quickly.

He brought them their ale drinks, their desired fancy napkins, resisted their childish insults, served their spiced foods, and even ate their leftovers when alone. Wood was needed for the oven, and he went out back where some cords are.  With a single karate blow of the hand cut and splintered several dozen into kindling.  With apron on he assisted in the kitchen, cooking, pouring, and even tasting when the meat and potato stew is done.  A variety of breads and pies he brought out to their clamors and laughter.  He even fed the prisoners chained to the sturdy posts on the porch making sure they too received his fine service.  By their thanks and desperate gobbling, they did not expect to eat.  A deep gleam of thanks passed amongst them remembering Alack's size and features.  When it was all over and the Palasatro had left for the plantations further up the road, both Matilda and Alack sat on the stoop catching their breaths and wondering how they had gotten through it all.

"A job well done, Alack…" she saw him gulping down what the prisoners did not eat.  "Still the deep burning?  It never stops with you?"

"I live to eat, Matilda.  With me, it's an obsession, food and my stomach go way back."

"But your limbs and lower body, there's no bulge of fat."

"I burn it off as fast as I can swallow, that's why I can do the impossible with this."  He popped a massive bicep and bulging muscle.  "My eating makes me strong."

"We worked well as a two-party dance troupe.  To the cleanup and a counting of our blessings," she held up a hefty bag of Jupents.  "Ravashor Karta maybe hard on those who offend but generous to those he likes, our number is high on his list, Alack."

"Law is for two things, to honor the good and punish the wicked."

"Maybe as so…"

Azar Massar welcomed his visitor and his men as they camped in the numerous guest houses around the plantation. Both took up a relaxed position on the wide porch with archways, stucco coated walls, big bay windows and a virtual forest of sweet-smelling flowers. Various Noxi (slaves) and indentured workers tended the landscaping, the wheat, barley and corn fields. Grazing livestock made contented baying sounds from the southern pastures. Clanks and chopping sounds came from various buildings away from the main manor house as blacksmiths and carpenters fashioned what was needed. Occasionally, the cracking of the Overseers whip and the pleading of his victim is caught on the warm breeze coming in from the northern fields.

Azar's manor is one of hundreds of immense sizes, almost self-sufficient, exporting more than importing to the big cities along the coast. Called 'Laughing Pines', Azar's family carved out an almost independent country on Vatados a century ago. They killed off the carnivore predators, enslaved the wild native inhabitance and cut down the forests, drained the swamps, to build a miniature community from untamed territory. Azar's grandparents, ambitious and considered insane, took on this challenge and built 'Laughing Pines' into a showcase for many other pioneers to follow.

"My great grandfather had a witty worded verse he would use, 'when you're not afraid of working hard you achieve a goal'. You're looking at that goal, Karta."

The Ravashor hoisted his fruity drink in a salute. "A fine goal made for the glory of the Shuton." His one good eye is alive and happy.

"How was your trek? Caught many fine fellows for my fields?"

"A low tally, Azar. But all are strong and sturdy, my men have them chained by the well. A good lot we arrested, but not as good at what I saw at the Inn at the Cross." Karta angled in to speak in a whisper. "Old Matilda has a fine young lad, a giant of muscle and long dark hair, of great strength from the North." Azar stopped sipping his drink, his wandering mind giving vent to Karta's words. "One of my men saw him chopping wood with his fist only. Whole cords fell as splinters at his feet. What powerful legs and upper body, a virtual champion from the tall rocky woodlands."

"You say he is well built? Long auburn hair and a boyish face, and great strength?"

"Yes…you know of such a lad?"

Azar went back to sipping his drink, his eyes following a water tank truck far off on the grassy knolls, his mind wandering off into past memories. "Sounds like a scoundrel I drove off world, Karta. I evaded him too often and he tried to arrest me on bogus bullshit, but I got the better of him. It pays to stay one foot ahead of your predator. If he comes back, they have his biometrics at the Space and Jet Ports…"

"Bio-metrics?"

"His DNA, flesh prints, Kirlian signature, stuff you would know if you're Ravashor in one of the great cities, but out here, things are simple, sweet and nice. This guy would be apprehended the moment he pisses on our soil." Azar gave the Ravashor a good warm grin. "You say he's strong and powerfully built?"

"He's a big Lad, from the mountains up north, Masalotus area, Village of Twin Falls, he claims the Iron Fist clan. They come down from the mountains to do feats of strength at seasonal fairs to earn money and get a wife…maybe…maybe he can be of use?"

"Yes!  I think I know that place.  I have some Noxi from that region."  Azar scratched under his wicked chin, "the Balaska Ball nearly upon us, maybe I'll hire him for some…entertainment?"

"And are not me and my good men invited?"

"Depends on how much you charge me for your prisoners, Karta?"


Alack finally tackled a daunting task at the Inn at the Cross.  Matilda showed him a dozen iron cooking utensils that have, over the years of use, become bent and useless.  To buy new ones would cost a fortune but Alack examined each one then smiled giving her ruddy face a pleasing goofy grin.  "If it's good for the septic system it's good for me…" he held up a long iron poker that became bent over the usage of time.  "Watch this!"  Spiking his metabolic rate for a second twisted the rod of iron into a straightness it had lost long ago.  Carefully powering down his heart so as not to burn off too many calories presented it to her.  "We aim to please, fair Lady."

"Such a persistence of might!"  She gestured at a table full of items, "If you please."

As she left Alack carefully began to straighten, to flat and make right her useless culinary utensils.  The last item, a long oddly bent fireplace spit rod, she wanted to be made into a 'U' shape for hanging heavy pots. Hoisting it on his broad shoulders Alack inhaled.  His naked torso expanding in a rib popping and sinew creaking affair made his heart beat three times faster, sending wave after wave of enhanced Seminian adrenaline throughout his powerful limbs.  In a slow titanic, steady throbbing of biceps, the massive bar bent to his muscular designs.

A softening of the rock hardness of his arms ceased as he made an almost perfect horseshoe of the rod.

"Now that be a display worthy of a crowd!" came a boastful voice from several men approaching. Dressed in green garments resembling a tunic affair with straps and belts, they approached. "Matilda said you be found in the back, but nothing as impressive as this!" Alack quickly grabbed his shirt as he powered down his heart. "Why cover what must be seen? Zounds such a display is pleasing and outright unusual to behold, Alack of the Iron Fist Clan."

"You have me at a disadvantage Sirs?"

"I am the Editar from 'Laughing Pines', I serve the one who sent me to find the one who chops wood with his fist."

"For what purpose is this about?" Alack scanned his mind, and the returning impression was only to serve by obeying his orders.

"He who is our Lord and Master at 'Laughing Pines' wants you to entertain his guests at the gathering feast for the Balaska Ball on the morrow." He held out a bag of Jupents jiggling in a seductive manner. "He who sent me can be most generous if complying."

"And if I refuse, good Sir?"

"No harm will befall you, but the future in these parts can be frightfully unpredictable."

"Fortune is the most unstable of all things…" muttered Alack. He made a funny grin. His luck is with him. With the ends of his lips up, he complied. "I will accept your sack Sir…" Alack went to take it but the crafty Fellow moved his hand away.

"Full payment after the festivities. Be at 'Laughing Pines' on the early morrow for instructions. As not to offend the guests, use the servants and Noxi entrance beyond the front gate.  Good day to you."

After they left Alack mumbled, "Now what was that all about?" Obviously one of the Ravashor's men saw him chopping wood with a martial art's strike on each cord.  Impressed told his boss, who told the plantation's Lord during a conversation, and this delegation happened to arrive when he was bending iron with his bare hands.  'This is good timing,' rethought Alack, 'maybe I can find Azar Massar at this feast or learn where he is.  According to scant information, he dwells at one of these plantations in the southern lands of Kornupa County.'  Deciding to test the waters of chance, Alack made a firm commitment to pursue this opportunity.

The next day, Alack packed away his traveling items in a sack, attached a wooden pole to the end.  His rustic tunic, disguised as a utility belt, heavy socks, and leathery brown boots, gave him a pioneer look. All he needed was leather pants, a hat made of fur from some forest critter to fulfill the proper image.  Not since the Wilderness Affair, or the Kudor Thor Affair, did he feel as such.  Taking a deep breath, he felt the leather twine stretch and pull the heavy fabric over his chest, then placed a deadly hunting knife, his feared Bowie, in its rightful holder on the belt.  Picking up his pole, angling it over his broad shoulder, turned towards the door of his room.

"Leave you not till my lips gives you a parting smack!"  Matilda is upon him pushing a heavy bag into his hands.  "The trek to 'Laughing Pines' is only an hour away by carriage but those big feet will require a half a morning at least."

The smell of cooked meats and breads drove his taste buds to new heights. "Thank you, good Lady, but I will return after the festival." Even though Alack had stuffed himself like the splendid pig he is, this spiked a deep hunger threat below.

"You brought better fittings than those I hope, they be the Magnita of the Lands you shall meet."

"I have a fine wardrobe within, Matilda…"

"Oh…you washed, but when you arrive, they have another perfumed bath, they have noses up in the clouds."

"Don't worry, I've got the soap you gave me."

"If the meat pies go bad use the Carcoca spice to kill the mold."

"I know all the herbal stuff you taught me."

"Remember, they be the Magnita, they go back ways into our ancestors past."

"I will be courteous, rest assured."

"I can close the Inn and be at your side…"

Deciding to end this, he gave her a gentle hug, "Keep open the Inn, you must serve the guests, Matilda. I fixed everything and more, I will be back." With a loud exhale, he set off down the ruddy pebbled road.

During his walk under the thick forests canopy the cobblestones and patches of cement of the road Alack has a moment to think. 'If I find Azar Massar amongst the guests, then what do I do? I just can't call in the SSG, which is normal police procedure. I've got to collar him and bring him to the Amazian Embassy in Waltsba City, but how do I do that? I'm out in the wilds here, no modern transport, nothing, but this crude road and primitive life style.' As his mind raced down corridors, opened doors seeking answers, realized he must wait and play this game out.  The right opportunity will rear itself, only he must be astute enough to recognize it and grasp the situation before it runs away.

The forest quickly gave way to a sudden open plain.

Alack paused, looking up.  A great weathered stone archway straddled the road where the forest ended.  He recognized the Raga-Noka.  A thick vertical 'I' with a horizontal bar cutting the center, and on both ends two ovals with half circles within, the old symbol of Unapiteria.  When the monarchy fell and a republic became reality, that symbol changed to the modern Raga-Hasa, a green oval with a horizontal bar bisecting it and ending with two verticals 'I's.  'Time is certainly standing still here', thought Alack, 'for two hundred and fifty years that old emblem had its heel on the neck of the entire galaxy; A vast engulfing tyranny that sucked away planetary wealth, funneling it all to the Magnita, the royal families, and the Celestial Monarch.  They had a simple system, they bought the planets raw resources for a pittance, chose special worlds for manufacturing goods and items, and sold them back at high, ridiculous prices.  But, in the first one hundred and fifty years, taxis were low and a degree of freedom did exist.  The slogan 'marentos de Vatados' (glory to Unapitar) was song in praise for the unity they achieved.'

'They did give us a sense of universality,' thought Alack as he studied the faded chiseled writing of a dead civilization.  'Before them there was chaos and the unknown.  We owe a lot to their 'stellar enlightenment' and the spread of art culture wherever they conquered, plus a fairly good legal system the Great Code is based upon.  Only within their last fifty years did they screw up and caused the Amazians to revolt.  When they started to change the original planetary charters and treaties to suit their own greed, then their downfall began. Too much wealth that isn't shared causes decay from within, says J. Wackon. A lesson I hope we've learned…' With that lingering thought, Alack pressed onwards to the vast, stretching cultivated fields below.

As the road became well paved, small trees and bushes lined the way as rolling fields of reddish and yellow Turnolves flowers covered the grounds as a giant beatific carpet. A wonderful, rosy sweet scent permeated the air. Some strange tingling sound of glassy fairytale winds whistled through dangling chimes as the flowery fields changed to crops and vegetables. The naked backs of Noxi slaves and indentured workers bent amongst the arrays of irrigation. An occasional 'crack' of a whip followed by the painful yelp of a dull-witted child made Alack frown, 'even amongst such loveliness there is this evil. The ways of God are just but the ways of men are unjust.'

He recalled the ancient Seminian philosopher Torrasho, whose theories on morality were taught to him by his mother. 'She believed in the Tork and the Pang, an almost round oval of white and black dividing it in half. In the Tork part is a black triangle, in the Pang part a white dote, meaning that even amongst goodness there is a touch of existing evil, the same opposite exists on the other side, creating a balance in all-natural creation…' The loud crying of a teenage girl under the lash caught his full attention. "Except for us!"

With a burst of revulsion, Alack grabbed a louse stone from the road's side and sent it flying like a missile. It struck the Taskmaster with such force the shard went through his body, splattering the adolescent with blood. Screaming in fear ran off as the body fell hidden amongst the melons and Somaka fruits. A sudden shock fell upon the workers as if time ceased and all lost a natural animation. One Slave saw the bloody pebble, scooped it up and hid it in his pocket as a token souvenir.

As shocked eyes fell upon him, Alack quickly hurried on his way.

The incident sparked his mind to a new height of reasoning.

'What if Azar Massar recognizes me at the party? He's seen me several times, close up. I'll have to play dumb, too late for makeup or grafting, play it by second sight...' Alack had a small woolen cap to hide most of his long hair and took a moment to put it on, then headed towards the side entrance as the main gate appeared.

A Guard stopped him. "And where by Paszsian you think your feet are going?"

"The Editar of the feast requested me, Sir."

"You're from the Inn at the Cross?"

"Yes, Matilda is the lady of the House."

He picked up an old-style telephone from the Guard's booth. "That guy from the Inn is here...okay." The Guard went to the servant's gate and unlocked it. "Go in, a fellow in a brown cloak with a whip is waiting, he's the Editar."

"Thank you..." and Alack quickly made a fast pace in through the wooden gate.

Thinking of the whippings Alack trudged up the beaten earth road to a series of storehouses and workshops. He heard the grinding of stones, the clink and clang of beaten metal, the cutting of wood and smelled the overwhelming sweet odor of baking bread. A wave of unreal hunger seized his inners as his taste buds began to burn and make tyrannical demands. The food Matilda gave him had vanished long ago.

"You with the body…come here." The same man who accosted him at the Inn the other day snapped his knuckles in a joyous pose. "I knew he'd come…" said the Editar to four others approaching, "They can't resist a few Jupents and our baker's craft." He jabbed the whip's handle at Alack's handsome startled face. "You think he's good for fucking?" The whip pointed to Alack's crouch area, a slight bulge parting his shorts. "I think I know a good bitch who would love to suck on that!"

Alack frowned, "I'm here as requested." His voice strained.

"Don't get heated my big muscular friend, just a little teasing to get the dust out, glad you're here. Welcome to 'Laughing Pines', the finest plantation in Kornupa County." He reached up and placed his hand on Alack's broad shoulder, the whip dangling down over his powerful stiff chest stretching the rustic shirt. "Relax, were not going to harness you to a plow, you are our guest, come, sit have a fruit drink." They gently led him to a picnic bench and Alack sat. As glasses and a cool pitcher brought around, he sent his mind out, read the impressions and confirmed their intentions; nothing devious, only curious and how to fit him into the show. "The Ravashor says you're from the mountains, way up north, Masalotus Province. Your villagers are iron and metal workers, right?"

Alack continued to study them as he sipped the sweet lemon drink. "The Grand Metazar of my village taught me the forge and the anvil…" Alack held up his two big hands making a powerful knuckle sandwich. "I am Alack, of the Iron Fist, a member of a special Clan of artisans and warriors."

"He maybe of some use around here, Boss." said one of the

Fellow's.

"I can't make that decision, but we'll try. What brings you to the southern latitudes, Alack?" The Editar fingered the brads on his whip, his mind further studying Alack's incredible upper body development. "No bother, just glad you're here, trying to figure what work you can do during the festival other than entertain?"

"That's what I wanted to talk about…"

Before any other can make a suggestion a dozen sweaty Noxi laborers ran over. Breathing hard the lead Guy removed his hat and spoke, panic rising in his fast tongued voice. "Sorry Boss Guy but we need help! Taskmaster Will do locked in an ice house, can't get out, he freezes in there! We need help!"

Everyone jumped up, including Alack after he drained the pitcher, and ran after the group. They came to a metal and brick box structure of one story, a heavy bronze door in the front is the only entrance. The Editar jingled the locking mechanism, saw it is broke, and turned to the Laborer. "You turned off the coolant?"

"Yes, Boss Guy, but without the door open not venting…he's gon'na freeze!"

"How long ago?"

"A only fifteen minutes or so…"

"We've got to get this door off…" The Editar and his men studied the hinges but the door opens from the inside, not from the outside. "We need sledgehammers…lots of'em and many hands…lots of…"

"I think I can help." Calmly approached Alack removing his tunic and belt, "I am of the Iron Fist, I know all metals, their strengths and weakness…" He began feeling the studs of the metal plates, the small corrosion of the bronze sheets, and after a few minutes turned towards the others, determined. "I can do this, watch!" Flexing his massive upper body in a powerful tensile bursting display of muscle and sinew, Alack made a gigantic fist. Spiking his metabolic rate, found an area where the iron bolts are badly rusted, and drove his knuckles into the bronze plate. It bent inwards, through rotten inner wood insulation. The corroded iron bolts popped out as Alack's long powerful fingers enlarged the hole. Eyes went wide as he grabbed the exposed section of the door, and in one mighty yank of back sinew and straining deltoids, the heavy door left its frame and collapsed to the ground.

Everyone jumped back, their eyes glaring in shock.

Alack took one massive breath, stretching straining his chest and ribs, and powered down his adrenaline and beating heart to Seminian norms.

The Laborers are already inside helping the Taskmaster out.

One Asshole Cleric remarked, "Your gon'na pay for that!" and ran off.

The laborers and slaves, who liked the Taskmaster, began to congratulate the huge, muscular guy. Their faces lit up, big smiles showing dirty teeth, a brightness seldom seen in such a hostile place. As Alack yanked on his shirt, he saw the hope rising against the destitute in their hungry eyes, and a germ of an idea fermented. 'Maybe…' he thought, 'maybe…but it's a long shot…'

A hand fell upon Alack's broad shoulder, the fingers not to honor but to grab, caught his attention. "Sorry but come with me," said the Editar in an almost embarrassed tone. Three other Taskmasters, with menacing whips and hanging truncheons from their belts, stood behind him with an ugly frown. "Go with these men and cause no trouble."

The hairs at the nape of Alack's neck tingled danger. He sent his mind out and felt their impressions, one of anticipated brutal delight.

Deciding to obey, Alack allowed them to take him to a shack in the woods called the 'school room'. Was he recognized as the one who hit the Taskmaster in the field? He will soon find out. On the walk there, he felt many eyes on him from the workers in the field and common laborers. By their terrified looks, they knew his future from past ordeals. Going inside, the same Cleric who saw him tear off the icehouse door, instructed the three men to prepare their instruments. Alack saw a cauldron of red-hot charcoal with pokers heating up. Another Taskmaster was removing a heavy chain off the wall and testing its links, the third guy removed a deadly cat-o-nine tails from a dresser draw.

"Get your shirt off, hear!" Screamed the Cleric trying to sound domineering, but his voice is more of a mere lady like scream than a beasty growl.

Alack obeyed.

He can withstand the whip, the chains, but the hot pokers would really hurt. Even though his body will heal itself quickly, the idea of burning flesh revolted him. Stiffening, ready to spike his metabolic rate and resist. Alack eyed them menacingly.

As the three Men stood ready, another Guy ran into the room, whispered something into the Cleric's ear, "He was killed in the fields?" The Guy nodded 'yes', both paused in surprise, they made a flash decision, and ran out. The three Men, holding their torture instruments ready, glanced at another. They decided to wait, expecting the Cleric to return and begin the torture. But, after fifteen minutes, he never returned. The poker cooled, the chain got heavy and the whip went limp. Feeling depressed and rejected, they put their items away and walked out grumbling.

Alack found himself alone.

"Now what was that all about?" He mumbled putting his shirt on.

Azar Massar sat on the veranda sipping his cool lemonade while four Servants stood ready to receive orders. He delegated to each one certain items for the big party in the evening. As the three left to carry out his demands, he used his scepter to restrain the forth Servant. "Here's a special guest list. Make sure they get anything they want, including the Inamorato and his wife the Inamorata, give them my quarters in the backyard grand house, I'll sleep in the empty servant's quarters, the one who died in the fields."

"They…the planetary Shutons…here at the estate?" the Man's eyes went wide.

"You think I throw a low-class affair? Our two love birds need more diversions these days, the more we give them, the more freedoms we have. This will enhance my status for a future career on Vatados, my good servant, and know this, if I go up you might go with me and even gain your freedom, no strings attached." The Man bowed delighted. "You've been the best out of the six who serve me. You make the Noxi sink and tremble with your passing, and you're not afraid to use the whip, I've heard stories, good stories, from my Overseer."

Avar poked the Man in his Eaton vest with the scepter. "Also, but tell no one, the Lady Inamorata, I need a chance meeting. Something that is accidental and I come to her rescue…something not to threatening but serious enough to warrant a good response." Azar studied the Fellow, who is now bubbling with ambition.

"Maybe Lord a diversion to scare? I will work on this and consult."

"Ha! Good boy, I can smell a most plentiful future if you succeed." Azar took him by the shoulder and walked around, whispering into his eager ear. "Pay close attention. When their flying machines arrive, collect all the starter pads and give them to a trusted fellow of your choosing. Dress him in fancy clothes, he'll be our valet."

"Yes Lord, a capital idea, very exclusive and royal! He will remember what belongs to who?"

"Star shit! Once they land give the box with the pads to me, I won't let them leave until certain demands are meet, understand."

"Oh yes, a pretty scheming time this evening!"

"Now go, my Editar waits."

He exited as the Editar took up his position by the table. "I've figured out a simple entertainment using the Big Lad from the Inn at the Cross, Master. What I planned will be received and make this Ball a remembrance for many years."

"I expect no less. Masa Avallania, the Themis of Waltsba City will arrive by Zo car with his group. We need to find a place for him to land with the others, that area over by the West Wing must be cleared and made presentable. Get some Noxi and work them."

"Yes, I know the patch, but those boulders and trash may need many hands."

"Our muscle Lad from the Inn, offer him a bonus if he assists, I heard about the Ice House rescue, impressive..."

"Just wait and see him at the Ball, Master." The man rocked on the heels of his boots with pride. "He'll prove his worth in golden manure."

"Have you found the killer yet?"

"No, Master, but it was done with a sharp pebble. I think one of the Noxi has a sling shot weapon and used it. There's a bad feeling going around..." He leaned in over the table whispering. "Methinks something extra for the Noxi and indentured workers will be in order to smooth things out?"

Azar hoisted his drink looking away in arrogance. "So now I must cater to the scum?" He looked at his cool, refreshing glass of lemonade. "Do we still have that keg of Beetle Wine in the basement?"

"Uh...yes, it's probably vinegar by now, but I think it's still there."

"Break it open and sweeten it. Let them suck it down, that bile will not sour in the stomachs of my property, they've had far worse." The Editar broke a nasty grin. "Put Ravashor Karta and his men in certain places to keep order, just in case we have a few bold ones. I don't want Quadralane to know of this."

"That rodent of a school teacher shows his face here to make trouble. I'll stamp the life from his ugly, tiny body!"

"Now, now, now, we must have a necessary evil in paradise. It makes us look okay."

Within an hour, the entire estate staff of house servants is jumping and running about getting things ready at the manor house. Guest rooms are cleaned and freshened, master bedrooms and other chambers are made bed perfect for a flood of guests. Most of the house butlers and laundry maids sacrificed their quarters so more guests could have a comfortable place to sleep. As chandeliers are dusted, furniture is polished, and rugs cleaned, Laughing Pines becomes a great big bed and breakfast for the two-day festival. Trucks arrived from other estates with beverages, exotic foods and candies of a sumptuous variety.

And it is in the kitchen that the Editar finally finds who he is looking for.

"Iron Fist Boy, are you still eating?"

"What I brought wasn't enough, Sir, and the delicious odors just drove me in here." Grinned Alack finishing off the leftovers the master chef dared not feed to the Magnita. "Is there anything I can do for you?"

"Well said, if a full belly makes you compliant, I'll give you more later. Come, walk this way." Alack followed the man to a large debris filled piece of flat land behind the manor house. Small boulders, shattered masonry, wood splinters, and broken glass littered the whole area. Once used as a dumping ground for non-bio garbage, it was abandoned when recycling was introduced. A flat under layer of bricks is covered by a good twelve Illos (half a foot) of grass and hard sod. Two dozen slaves and laborers stood ready with shovels, rakes and brooms off to the side. "This area must be cleaned down to the flagstones beneath, you, Iron Fist are to supervise and add your hands to theirs if need be. I've got other things to do than watch you sweat and complain. Two hours from now, my eyes expect to see a clean flat tarmac for parking flying cars from the capital and beyond." Without any more talking, the Editar jabbed his whip at Alack's chest and pointed it to the job area. The gesture told the others who the boss man is. He turned and left the work sight.

Pleased at his good fortune, Alack had wondered how he would get his plan motivated too action? The Editar has now done it for him.

Commanding the laborers to begin, they began removing the debris and litter around. Some pieces are large broken cement brick and mortar chunks, which Alack hoisted and rolled off the area rather than getting a cart and more workers. As they pulled off the thick growth of sod Alack noticed the Laborers constantly watching him. Their eyes spoke of eagerness restrained by patience. Knowing their expressions, Alack sent his mind out and received impression confirming their secret desires. Eventually, one husky Fellow started digging with his shovel within earshot.

"We saw what you did to Taskmaster."

Hoping for one of them to come forward Alack began to lay the framework of his plan. In low whispers, he gave the young Fellow eye contact. "He was beating a harmless child, I hate that. Why did you allow it?"

"Boss Master to strong, we are too weak to resist." came a sad grumble.

But Alack felt the strained anger in his tone. "The heart of a hero is never too weak. You are many, they are few, make your demands or revolt. This whole system is wrong and you know it."

His shovel struck the flagstones beneath with a clang of frustration. "We be chained by the law. We made our misery and must pay for it this way." He nodded towards the others working around them.  "We all criminals and must serve out our sentences by beating and hard labor, nothing to be done."

"I understand.  Yes, you all have a price to pay, but it must not be harsh like this, or brutal on your children.  There are more humane ways of doing justice than the whip and lash of the taskmaster, my friend.  This system takes away your dignity as free men, replacing it as caged animals."

"Free men, once we be that, but fault our own, we make this hell by our past actions, but methinks you are right.  There are better ways than pain and a broken back.  Quadralane's words are a fire of hope."

"Who is this Quadralane?"

"Great teacher who wanders lands in secret, spreading hope for the Noxi.  Giant foot prints he treads, and the Magnita tremble in his wake."

'So…' thought Alack, 'there is a resistance…'  Making decision Alack explained who he really was and what he must do to get Azar Massar collard and in jail.  "I have a plan, and I think if we all work together on this, not only can I get what I want but you guys can get a fair deal for justice.  But we must act fast.  Tonight, is the big party and everything must be ready at a precise moment to win, otherwise, nothing changes and the misery continues.  Do you agree?"

A long moment of silence ensured between them.  Only the diggings of the Man's shovel added substance to the long wait.  Finally, the dirt activity stopped.  "We have a secret…between other farming estates…runners send messages, we be organized.  I can call many, a mighty host of men with pickaxes and forks, to assemble here and make demands."  He gave Alack a determined frown, "Quadralane is big leader. He called Shamanasta, the giant one. He'll come and bargain for us. Say word and shall be done."

"The bravest of men fear nothing!" Relieved, animated, Alack broke into a happy grin showing all whites. "Many important people will be here at midnight. This is the time to act!" Feeling a deep trust has been earned, Alack took a daring chance and handed the Man his Special Service ID card he gives to those to entice. "Have your big giant leader see this, he'll understand and know the time is here. We are in earnest. A chance like this may never come again!" And Alack explained the further details, the precise timing of his plan.

That evening, they arrived in droves.

The open tarmac is packed with Zo Car from a variety of years, one sleek as a recent model the others older but of renowned luxury. Several Silorian (road) vehicles are parked in another open area by the manor house, and in all, about two hundred of the planet's finest Magnita ever been seen under one roof. The great hall is crammed to overflowing. All guest rooms plus finer servant quarters are filled, and added supplies are brought in from the surrounding plantations by many slaves and indentured servants. It seems this annual Balaska Ball fell upon 'Laughing Pines' this particular year, which Azar Massar insisted upon hosting at his estate. But the real exciting couple is the Inamorato Shuton and his wife, Inamorata, plus his chief aides, the main attraction. With Vatados banners hanging and guests singing the anthem, the romantic couple entered to wild cheers and foot stomping salutes. Four finely uniformed Palasatro Guards flanked the procession with raised, polished partisan spears, with hidden photonic blasters.

Before they took their seats on the dais both embraced and began the first dance to commemorate the opening of festivities.  Famous for their seemingly elegant gliding steps, both in long flowing robe and gown, swung another in a sweeping swirling motion of precise enhanced moves.  The handsome Shuton, with his curling mustache and groomed beard, led in a dignified plucking of fingers over her shoulders and arms.  She, the Inamorata with a golden wig of glittering jewels from a priceless tiara, gently swooned back from his manly touch, her rosy face aglow in a lover's trance.  With unmasked affection they circled the polished dance floor for three turns, then the band went into a louder percussion and others joined in.

After fifteen minutes of structured dancing, the Master of Ceremonies banged his wooden staff and announced the first course is ready to be served.  All the pampered guests in their elegant waist coats and long consuming gowns took their respected seats at tables with old fashion candelabrums.  As Azar Massar, dressed to the hilt in a long blue waist coat with fancy gold trim and a red sarong with tassels, took his seat at the table with the Shuton party, two dozen acrobats and jugglers took the floor.

"Oh..." began the Lady Inamorata rubbing her bosom in recollection, "I remember this troupe from the last ball."

"Let me do the massaging," gleefully intoned the Shuton Inamorato, "my lips are hot and they want you!"

"Be not bored, Exalted Ones," added Azar Massar wanting to join in, "we have a special guest, from the ancient mountains of Masalotus, a mighty young man who will entertain."

"Masalotus? That province is within my jurisdiction," began one of the Aides, "two years ago we did a genetic history study and found the inhabitances are direct descendants of the original indigenous inhabitances of Vatados. And we thought they all died off from sickness…but they descend every so often to seek cattle and wives. I dare say some don't know the difference." His humor is lost.

"Are they big, muscular, with long hair?" asked Azar with a suspicious squint.

"Yes, and they're master iron workers of terrible, inhuman strength, but recluses, so we left them in peace." A seemingly release of a great weight passed from Massar's stern features. "You can read about them in the library archives."

Azar jerked his head back at the Aide, the look of suspicion returned with greater force, but he said nothing, clenching his teeth.

"My fingers fly at your cheeks!" The Shuton's reddish tongue leaped in and out like a canine over a treat. "Let me wait no longer your luscious pearl!"

"It's so hard for me to resist such entitlements."

"A fire burns my throat, and only you can put it out!"

"Some later time but not here…"

"My inners are twisting for your embrace!" He filled her wine glass drinking from it first before presenting it to her. "Every drop of your love is mine to drown in!"

"And I thought you would be better behaved once outside our chambers."

"No wall or mountain can stop my tidal rush!" A servant placed a golden plate of delicacies on a table in front of them. "Until now...methinks I'm hungry." And the planetary ruler began stuffing his face.

Masa Avallania the judge and his guests, seated next to Azar on the dais held up his goblet in salute, "A worthy demand from our Shuton! Time to indulge…"

Azar waved to the Master of Ceremonies when the acrobats finished.

Alack entered in silky red pants, black boots, a black sash tied around his slim waistline, an open vest that began just where his chest ribs jutted and a bag like hat that hid his long locks. With his hair tucked in he looked very different at that distance from the raised platform. Disguising his voice in a more baritone than his youthful tone, Alack introduced himself. He popped a few bicep surges with his forearm muscles, a powerful flexing of upper chest and deltoids, a few flips and areal gyrations, to a few martial arts moves of incredible dexterity. Then he asked for the volunteers to bring out his items.

The Ravashor Karta came out with a few of his men lugging heavy chains, an iron bar for prying up boulders, and a large wooden trunk from a cut tree.

"He's a virtual giant," commented the Aide, "I knew they are large but not that large. None of our ancient diseases can kill his type."

"Does he look familiar, Masa?" whispered Azar squinting at the judge.

"Not one bit, who be you thinking of?"

"That annoying Servie you drove off planet."

"I think you are imagining too deeply, Azar. He's gone far and wide back to Amazia and its haunts. Even vermin must hide."

Azar frowned knowing his gut instincts were to be trusted, not ignored.

For his first feat of strength, Alack had them tie the heavy chains around his chest. When done a guest from one of the tables came up to examine the links. Agreeing they are proper and real, Alack told everyone to stand back. Spiking his metabolic rate pumped huge volumes of adrenaline into his system. Feeling a vast rush of energy swelling his muscles, inhaled, expanding his barrel chest. As all eyes opened in wonder, the Boy's tensile tan skin stretched, turning a nasty red. A metallic screeching filled the silent room as Alack's torso strained under further growth. In a sudden burst, a splat of metal grey links showered the audience. Like dead twigs, they rolled and clinked over the wooden floor. A loud applause followed as Alack powered down his heart to save on calories.

"What a performance…" began the Shuton, going back to his main course, "this is cold, bring me another." He caught the lovely round complexion of the Queen. His wasted eyes fell upon her lusty breasts, the mustache, and the goatee pointing. "Hello Boys, I'm back…and I missed you!" She giggled and swooned as he plunged his face between her cleavage, "My tongue tickles till dawn…"

"Oh…such a display…Shutykins!"

"If you liked the jugglers, you'll love this!"

Alack held up his hands, showing off his palms and was given the iron heavy bar. Holding it out, going to the front table allowed the guests to touch and study it. Satisfied it is genuine he took his place back in the floor's center. Taking a few breaths, Alack spiked his metabolic rate for a second and twisted the iron shaft into a pretzel. More applause, even some shouting, now followed as he brought his body down to its norms.

"If those original people had such strength…" mumbled the Aide, "how did we conquer them four hundred years ago?"

"With this…" said the Ravashor pointing to his polished side arm after he returned from the floor, "and iron men in rickety space ships."

"My ancestors had that pioneering spirit," added Azar trying to make a decision over who the Strong Man really is. "They knew the odds and weren't afraid of the dangers. Anyone can bend iron but to have it in your belly is another matter."

"Well said, Azar." And Masa Avallania the Judge, toasted him.

For Alack's last act, two of Ravashor's men held the thick cut tree trunk out, both facing one another but at a safe distance. Alack made an 'x' sign with his fingers along the center of the flat rings. Focusing a burst of concentration, seeing behind the bulky wood in his mind's eye, Alack let out a shout. He is so fast his lethal fingers dashed the trunk which splintered in halves. Both men stumbled back with the pieces as more clapping and shouts came from the guests. Alack smiled, waved, bowed, then made a hasty exit.

"Such display has made my hand seek a moment of joy…" The Shuton's greasy fingers began to paint with the gravy a red 'x' on the Queen's upper exposed nipples. "If X marks the spot, my tantalizing tongue comes to plunder!" Pushing aside his mustache, he slurped his way to her neck. "And sweetness abounds to the very top!"

"You're such an animal at these affairs…ohhh!" His face, tongue and lips are all around her soft neck. "Easy on your practice, Sweets, the room is real!"

"What's real comes at you now!"

"Theory and reality are two different things," Chuckled the Themis (judge) Avallania jabbing Azar Massar in his side. "Ever pry the lid to those on Amazia?"

A moment of diversion brought Azar back to his current guests. "Yes. But they aren't so crude on Amazia. There's this silly cultural thing called Victonian that restrains and makes fucking seem like a lace curtain blowing in a flower shop. You can't do this or say that or have any fun, returning to Vatados is a fresh breath of air for me, Masa. Here I can do what I want."

After his show of strength, Alack became ravenous so fast and deep, he began grabbing leftovers from the returning dinner plates. Glasses of half-filled wine and beverage drinks satisfied his thirst. When two dish washer slaves came to get the carts, the servants left by the kitchen, Alack made a pleasing burp pointing. "You don't have to wash them." Feeling light headed made a hasty exit outside. A Slave in fancy waist coat and ruffles showed him a rosewood cigar box. "Thank you but I don't smoke lung weed or takes drugs from Sweet sticks..."

"Oh no, Sir, these here and within are key pads to flying machines."

"Alack paused, his mind reeling from the fast intake of different alcohols quickly snapped into high gear remembering. "Let me see that..." Opening the sweet-smelling aroma of the box saw a dozen electronic starter pads. Recognizing one, took it. "A Starleg Cosmar A1000...I know this model."

"That be the Themis of Waltsba's machine!"

Alack made a goofy, delighted grin, "don't hesitate not to vegetate…" and thanked him, giggling. "Where force can be used law is not needed." Alack watched the fellow carry the box to Azar Massa on the dais, he is ready to act.

"I'm awash by the sparkles of your face." The Shuton's puckering lips made obscene sucking kisses under and behind the Queen's neck. "Wait! My pretty prize, and see how many I can offend before the late evening ends."

His menstruation and whiskers made her blush and giggle. "Oh Shutykins…what will others think?"

"A jealous fool will only watch, a better fellow will admire, and a great man will copy…my tongue a torpedo of love!" He is all over her as the others enjoyed the romance of the high royal luminaries.

"If only those under our heel can be as that," sighed Masa Avalliana, "my job will be as a death sleep under a warm sun, whose rays will give both hands a shaking."

"A riddle?" Azar suddenly paused as a fresh delightful idea shot into his craven brow, and looked over at the fancy uniformed Ravashor. "Did your men find the killer of my taskmaster?"

"At this time, Lord Azar, a loss I am at, but my investigation continues."

"Did you find the murder weapon?" Grinned in a sadistic manner.

"No, but a theory is had, based upon the arrival at the same moment the death occurred. I am thinking the strong Fellow from the Inn may have done it, but there is no evidence I have as yet."

"You mean…" began the Judge Avalliana, "a felon goes

unpunished?"

"We need to seek and arrest the murderer, Lord High Themis." answered Karta.

"Why bother with formalities. You are the Ravashor in this province, arrest them all. Use the ten percent decimation rule, terror is its own justice."

"I've heard of that one." Azar put his quick devious scheme to play, and ordered the Master of Ceremonies to bring in the Strong Man. "We'll settle this the old way, but with a new twist. Evidence? Who needs evidence, just find an example."

Ravashor Karta stood clutching his polished, bulky blaster and gave the order to his men to assist the Master of Ceremonies, his one good eye enjoying the sudden change.

"Under the Law," began Avalliana whispering in Azar's ear, "just one word of confession is needed. A single word of self-guilty spoken, and another wretch will dangle in the breeze." A sinister giggle moved his features in delight. "And if you think that upstart from Amazia, who has trodden in secret, returns, we'll use the Nosh Vis'blk, our hidden tongue to confound him and trap him to the gallows."

"You are such a breath of fresh legal air. Here he comes now."

Alack sent his mind out as he re-entered the quiet chamber. The impressions he now received are not good. A sinister, invisible weight has fallen like a black curtain. It choked out the gaiety and replaced the light feeling with a heavy noose. A malevolent expression is awash over Azar's face, which slowly beams with utter satisfaction for revenge. Realizing he must have seen through his disguise, Alack decided on a strong defense with the truth.

But for the other, the Judge Avalliana, his impression is deeper. A murky pit with swirling designs and a web took on a deadly purpose in Alack's mind. For some reason of instinct, this fellow is far more dangerous than Azar is. A saying came to mind as Alack stood before them, 'fear not outward appearance but the subtle designs within'.

"Wonderful Magnitas and added luminaries of Vatados, we shall test our strong man from the mountains of Masalotus not with muscles of his arms but the grey stuff of his brain. As in olden times when our ancestors ruled the galaxy from Unapiteria, I shall present to him a riddle. A popular saying from the misty hills and deep mines of his province, I charge you to answer." Azar Massar stood up and thrusted a finger at Alack. "A youth climbed the Baramore tree to gather its nuts, he worked at it all day but had nothing to show when he returned home."

A rumbling of throats passed around the room until one guest shouted. "I know! He ate them all! I win!"

"That's not the answer," squinted Azar Massar glaring down at Alack.

Realizing whatever he says or does he is unmasked, answered the riddle. "The Baramore doesn't make nuts, only the Sayamore tree does."

"So, Alack Troyus, we meet again," began Azar gloating over his brainstorm of detective work. Returning to the dais, he took his goblet, sipping his wine, "how you got back here doesn't surprise me, recalling how resourceful you are, but what concerns me you dare present yourself intending to arrest me. I refuse to be dragged back to Amazia and face my accusers. I have rights and privileges on Vatados."

With the two Palastro Guards flanking, Alack yanked off the

silly hat, shaking his long hair in defiance, and puffing up his bare chest while straining the lacing of his vest. "My authority is given by he who rules the Universe, Azar Massar, and I'll say this, before the rising of your sun you'll be in chains on your way to Amazia."

"A brave noise, Servie." His giggle evolved into a suppressing laugh. "If that's so, then I'll be kicking and scratching all the way to Newlon City."

"What handsome hair for a Noxi," intoned the delighted Inamorata.

At that moment, the fumbling face of the planetary Shuton glanced up from the bosoms of his lusty Queen. "Who's going to Amazia? Azar, what's this Noxian talking about?" The mustache and goatee are peaked.

"A rather minor off world matter, My Lord," answered the Themis Avallania, "this one has a brave impertinence to heave injustice upon our worthy and loyal citizen Azar Massar of Laughing Pines, for some fractions and violations stemming from a paltry crime going back years, hardly worth such a bundle of legal trouble, My Lord."

"Then pay the Noxi off and send him on his way." The Inamorato began to blow sweet bubbles between the nipples of the Queen from a pleasure smoking device. "Such a rude distraction on the festival day, shall we roll over and play judge or just roll over and play dirty, dearest?"

"Why wait, the jugglers were fun, and that strong slave is a delight, begin the trial."

"Say there, Avalliana, twirl your baton and let's have a court." He started to lick and pull on her ears. "This tongue wants more than a verbal twang!"

"Oh…Shutykins…you'll compromise the dignity of the bench?"

"My dignity was lost when I first laid eyes on you!"

"Be it as so," began the Themis of Waltsba City. "Once you stood before my high bench, Alack Troyus and sampled my justice, here a bout's matters play a different sway. The sanctity of my procedures is not followed in such a delightful setting as this, but our jurisprudence knows no bounds within, so I invoke the Nosh Vis'blk, a similar court procedure to your tribunal status, accept do you of this?"

Alack, who had the power of Consular Imperium, to pass judgment at any locality outside an official court under certain situations, gave his consent.

Azar Massar nudged Avallania in the side whispering. "We have the scoundrel."

"Not until he answers in the positive, condemning himself," hissed Avallania. "Ravashor Karta, would you please have the honor of recording these proceedings?"

"With my pleasure, most high Themis." He is given an old Calcomp.

"Use Linear H for court clerical purposes, if you please."

"What's that?" asked Azar Massar in a low, guttural voice.

"Proper translation codes… no error this time." Avallania faced Alack putting on his legal stern face for law enforcement. "Be it Knowned on this date, place and time, Alack Troyus of the Amazian Special Services stands again in judgment before the legal statutes of Vatados as guaranteed by the Code of Dwitinton and the Emperor of all the Amazians. That this proceeding is according to the wishes of the planetary Curlator and Shuton for clearing and expunging citizen Azar Massar of any criminal intent and past doings off and beyond the sacred soil of Vatados. So as according to our laws and unwritten customs, upheld by the Great Code and sacred Charter of Star Master Balaska in 1831 UT., this court is now in session." An aide gave Avallania a glass of sparkling golden wine. "Too many verbal bouts make's one thirsty." He took his time sipping. "Alack Troyus, explain to this ckovteun why you krahne an men bubbal vos nab citizen?"

Alack gave his right ear a gentle tug as his translator, for some weird reason, made a squeal, blinked out and back on over the first question. He had not heard this effect since the Tartarus Affair where a specialized corporate lingo was used. The returning language codex came back in a slightly different tone as the hidden device struggled with the Amazian translation. It said, 'explain to this court why you are incriminating a worthy man?' (What really Avallania said, 'explain why you're here as a criminal citizen?')

"Good people of Vatados, your Excellencies and Citizens under the Ring, my reasons are social crimes against honest men with good standing careers in public office. Azar Massar has corrupted and debased Amazian ethical codes and social values harming the innocent and abusing those who failed to do his will..."

Azar grinned, whispering, "are you getting this?"

Avallania made a gentle nod, "our translation is implicating him, not you. A name can be twisted as simply as a word. I've altered Linear H..." He held up a small recording device hidden in his wide cuff.

"My Affair has driven Massar off Amazia, leaving a trail of deceit and mayhem that has brought me here, to your fine planet, to collar him and return him to Amazia to face his accusers in a court of law.  But my efforts have been stymied and blocked.  Now, with your pleasure, I charge, I demand, in the name of our Emperor, you handover Azar Massar for criminal processing."

"Such a body kcoshem needs a retake kadash?"  Asked Avallania.

Alack's translation came out as, 'a refreshing of evidence' (what was actually said is, 'you must admit your guilt'.)  "You have my previous records on file from our last encounter, Judge Avallania."

"I see…but hozal of the damning a schowchet in field?"

Alack's translation came as, 'has criminal committed murder?' (What really said, 'do you know who killed the Task Master?')  "There is some evidence, your Honor, but it's still under investigation."

"It is skmar and smeir by you."

Alack's translation came out as, 'if so then death will be done.' (What said is, 'we think you killed the Task Master.')  "All that must be decided on Amazia, Sir."

"Ask him the question!" gagged Azar almost spitting in Avallania's ear.

"Patience…"  A look of finality washed over the Themis's stark face.  "Since la'ham arriving m'huoten vy laws, Alack Troyus?"

Alack's translator said, 'so, you think the accused is guilty of opposition?' (What really said, 'did you kill the opposing man in the field?')

"Don't answer, Colonel Troyus!"

A skinny, tiny figure came forward.  Dressed in a white flannel Nehru jacket, with a military utility belt, white pith helmet, the face was ruddy with a sun burnt youthful complexion, angled a walking cane at Alack. His piercing red eyes seemed to shock everyone in the room, especially Avallania and the Ravashor. The two Palasatro Guards looked dumb and questioned what to do now.

Behind the small stout brave Fellow over several hundred slaves, workers, and indentured servants pushed and shoved their way into the banquette hall. They separated in groups, standing behind every table, clutching something sharp beneath their smelly rags, and smiling with dirty teeth at the guests.

"Quadralane!" pointed out the Ravashor grabbing his holster while standing. "I want no trouble!" but did not draw the weapon.

"And I give none." He turned towards Alack, eyeing him up and down. "I see in you, my danger; coming here is worth the risk." The tiny, dark-skinned face stretched with dignity. "I am Quadralane, I represent those who are oppressed by the ruling Magnita on Luxdrew, or as you call this place, Alpha Vatados. Do not answer the Themis Avallania. He is using the ancient legal tongue of the Shutons. Your translator will not give you the real meaning of his words. By answering his question, you will implicate yourself and be arrested for murder. Your illegal stay on Luxdrew will end here and now. Your mission and life ends in failure."

With mouth hanging open, Alack sent out his mind and received a sincere impression. 'This is the giant leader?' thought Alack. 'He's a midget!'

"Who is this upstart who impedes the festivities?" The Queen broke a frown.

"He is the leader of the opposition in this province, Inamorata."

answered Azar eyeing Alack with renewed hatred. "My overseers at Laughing Pines and other Magnita estates have clashed heads with this rebel rouser."

"There is no opposition on Vatados." exclaimed Avallania in a restrained tone.

"Be there one or none, this Noxi seems to differ. Ravashor, what say you?"

"I know this man, Inamorato. He does command the Noxians all over the world. We have traded words in past encounters, but never has he committed a crime. He is a voice for those who labor for us. He has stood before the Magnita at your capital city and the centers of government in all the provinces, defending and pleading cases in the law courts. I would tread gently here, much badness can come of this if we don't."

"I agree with the local Ravashor, Inamorato," began his chief Aide, "what he says is very true. There are injustices he brings to court all the time."

"Why have these injustices not come before my eyes?" The Shuton's half sloshed gaze fell upon Avallania. "You know of these injustices?"

"They be a trifle matter, your Excellency, not to bother or annoy the beautiful Inamorata or your pleasures in governing."

"My pleasure in governing is afoul knowing my subjects are maltreated. What do you think, my Queen of the high couch?" All the time the chubby baby face of the Inamorato studied the events with unblinking eyes. Making a decision was whispered into Shuton's ear. "Oh…my fingers tingle with such wisdom…such warmth of your heart

I thought was only for me and myself." Licking her nose in a symbolic gesture of love, he returned to the people below on the dance floor. "Quadralane, if there is injustice in your eyes, I wish to remove it. We want a happy world, not a harmful one. I know our charter is chiseled in stone but stone can be remade, the writing redone. I have known we are a fraction of a sandy pebble on a vast shore that still has a slave institution. Let us work to change that."

Quadralane gave a lofty, deep bow. "I have waited and toiled many years for this day, Inamorato."

"Know also, what will be done here and today will not be an easy withdrawal of our laws over the Noxians but a…" his bloodshot eyes looked up, seeking the right word, only to have the Queen whisper it in his ear, "but an easing of such laws." Delighted with himself the Shuton broke a fine happy face, the mustache and goatee curling.

"I can't ask for anything else, Inamorato."

"Now isn't this nice…" he took the Queen's plumped hand. "The air in here has a rosy smell," he started to lick her fingers one by one, "and as such needs refreshing!"

"Your most high Excellency, shouldn't we consult…"

"Avallania, I want your resignation in the morning or my Palasatro will visit your estates and take what is pleasing." He caught the powerful image of Alack Troyus and recalled the previous. "Colonel Troyus, your accusations against Magnita Massar will be examined by my own legal counselors so there is no friction between US and the Capital of the Universe."

"I refuse it all!" yelled Azar leaping up and grabbing the Ravashor's blaster from his belt. In a forceful demonstration of defiance, he grabbed the Inamorata by her thick neck and collar pushing the cold hard nozzle under her chin. "Allow this, and the fat bitch becomes a headless corps!"

Everyone fell back in surprise and shock.

Those at their tables jumped up and screamed.

The four Palasatro Guards activating the close-range photonics of their feathered partisans. They stepped forward ready to start blasting away at the dais stage.

Ready for action Alack waved the Guards back as he came closer. A broad, amusing smile stretched his face. "And what are you going to do with that?" Alack started to giggle and point, the alcohol drinks still flushing in his veins.

Unnerved by this action, Azar swung around forcing the Queen to her feet. "You're not taking me, Servie..." but she is so fat he could not lift her and struggled.

Alack leaped.

A tumbling mass of muscles and hair, he flew over the frightened Inamorata. Azar angled the blaster up at Alack's twisting form. Depressing the trigger, the rusted antique broke apart into pieces. He landed behind Azar. "Give me that!" Alack tore the pistol remains from his grasp, and at the same time he pulled out his handcuffs from the utility belt and cuffed Azar Massar. "I arrest you in the name of the Emperor and people of Amazia. You have the right of trial by jury on this world or you may appeal to the Emperor. From this moment anything you say or do will be evidence against you."

"I appeal to the clemency of my own leaders!"

"You will not!" The Shuton gently seized his wife, leading her back in comforting caresses.  He saw the polished old style photonic pistol grip as the Ravashor took it from Alack.  "What bravery is within?  You do not fear the rays?"

"I knew that hasn't worked for years, Curlator."  Giggled Alack amused.

"Then my Lovely was never in any danger, but the act itself was evil."  The Shuton faced Azar with a threatening finger.  "You're actions of a desperate disposition proves your guilt, Azar Massar.  Let there be justice on Amazia.  Colonel Troyus, he is yours."  The Palasatro Guards and the Ravashor quickly escorted both world leaders out of the hall.

Quadralane, with a great sense of relief, smiled at Alack for bowing, and joined his aides in following the Shuton party out.

Alack seized Azar Massar by the shoulder.  His powerful fingers digging deep, tearing his fancy shoulder epaulets, "see, the sun is rising on a new world, or I'll give you a Seminian riddle.  Yes, my people can make one, 'shy yab, shy yurb, shy kurb, my rab!'  Means, very wise you are, very wise you be, very you are, but to wise for me."  Alack dragged Massar across the confused room to the back exit.  Finding Avallania's deluxe Zo Car tossed his prisoner in, jumped over the door and into the driver seat, used the key card to ignite the burners, vectored thrust and shot off and away.  Within an hour, as the sun climbed the horizon, Alack is landing at Waltsba City and the Amazian embassy.  Two hours later, a Special Service ship is on its way to Amazia.


"The Alack Effect..." mumbled T. A. Elanus as he painfully made grammar and spelling corrections to Alack Troyus's field report during the debriefing session.  The wiry gray haired old face continued to pucker and grimace as Alack sat quietly in the chair before his cluttered desk.

As the minutes stretched, Alack's Victonian posture slowly creped down to a lazy man's slouch. "What?" The handsome face erupted. The forehead wrinkling under the long flock of blackish to brown hair came alive. These long meetings after every assignment are a test for his impatient stamina. "You're talking to me?"

It is a loud exhale, not verbal. "My annoying after effects dealing with you when your finish stomping on worlds involving my assigned 'affairs'. But in this case the Alack Effect kicked in and left the place better off than when you arrived."

"You're talking about Vatados?"

"No, I'm talking about what they scratch on the walls in the lady's room. What you did at Laughing Pines is something Senator C. P. Aqualayon and his party had been trying to do for decades. It's called change. The old charter has been changed to do away with slavery, making it illegal. They still have an incarceration system that's antiquated but it's now more humane and along with modern Amazian standards."

"Wow!  Am I that good?"

"No. But you opened the door for Quadralane to work with the Shuton. They've instituted a better work program to pay off debts and serve time. The crimes are still on the books, but the harsh punishments have been altered. There's rehabilitation, the book has sort of replaced the lash, sort of." He finished off his corrections but hesitated in signing off on the report, making it official. "You did kill that Taskmaster, didn't you?"

Alack sat straight up. "I had to do something, Sir. He was beating a small child who would've died from his blows. If I threw that rock too hard, it was out of anger, not purpose."

"Then, the High Judge Avallania was right in his procedures."

"And I wouldn't be here, and your 'Alack Effect' would not have happened. First rule of achievement, nothing works smoothly."

"Alright, don't get testy on me, you did the right thing, Alack'm boy."

"The advantage is always with the people on the inside, but I beat them, I had to Sir, I had to find a way to get Azar Massar off Vatados as quickly as possible. This I achieved with great success. He has been accused, sentenced, and is serving time in a Corrective Colony, but! I have a complaint. I never got a full, in-depth briefing of Vatados and its legal setup. You never told me the SSG or Special Service has no authority there."

"Don't tell me what I know. You must learn to be a fool before becoming wise, you never gave me the chance. When I scheduled a briefing with Aqualayon and his people, you were gone, halfcocked and kicking ass all the way to Vatados. You were all revved up over the Telefona Affair, you weren't thinking." T.A. exhaled, pressing a button, and two glasses and a bottle of DeMassie wine rose up. He poured a small amount, activating the cold setting on the glass. "You ignored a direct order to leave Vatados. Other SSG agents obeyed, you didn't, why?"

"As you like to remind me, I'm Special Services. I'm very good in what I do. This guy really got under my thick Seminian hide." Alack took the glass, feeling the frosty layer forming, and changed the subject.

"The SSG doesn't toast their agents, they pin a medal on them instead." Alack made that funny smile with the ends of his mouth up.

"In some political circles, it's on their ass."

"The strong doesn't unsheathe their sword to win. But...your right, my success on the last Affair kind of...clouded my mind?"

"Speaking of that, when Azar threatened too shot you with Karta's gun, you laughed in his face, were you drunk or crazy?"

"I guess I never mentioned that antique stopped working years ago. He carried it only for show, and polished it for parties. I knew it wouldn't work when I first saw it. The inner mechanism was far gone, and when he pulled the trigger, it went to pieces." Alack swished the win in his glass as he deactivated the chilling mechanism built into the glass bottom. "DeMassie is best served at room temperature, or have you forgotten?"

"And...a good fart is good health, to quote you. Drink up, it won't kill you."

THE END

# THE SASHA DUNES AFFAIR

By Ernest Velon


They starved him for two days!

When the Zarbars thought Alack Troyus was too weak to resist anymore, they unchained him.  Once freed, he spiked his metabolic rate, crunched the needed calories, and wacked their boney heads together so hard, their brains splattered over his naked torso.  As the two Guards fell to their bare feet, Alack drove his muscular bulk through the stained glass window of the castle and felt sunlight and lacerations on his tensile skin.

Yes.  They denied him of precious food for agonizing days as they whipped and tortured his upper body.  But Alack had planned for the worse.  Not only did he gorge himself, but stashed a dozen expander pills in his underwear before arriving at the Zarbar fortress supposedly as the guest of the local Hebordar (warlord).  When alone, he popped a few into his mouth, the high protein mass exploded in his belly, maintaining his super human strength.  What was to be a hunting party turned nasty when Alack was betrayed by the female guide, who was supposed to be his companion.  She claimed he raped and seduced her with a magical spell, then stole her box of jewels and hid them in the forest.  Within this box was the priceless icon of the God Trulalar that will give the Hebordar of Guodwinsan ultimate power over his foes.  Alack's job is to steal this item and return it to the priests of Belox so the balance of power on Parbator III is maintained. So, peace can continue for another thousand years.

Starving, but not shaking, Alack powered down his heart rate saving calories as he plunged into the icy waters of the moat. Pumping wildly to the lower depths sought the rear side of the castle, which is not guarded as well as the front. Breaking the surface, found a place to crawl from the murky feces polluted waters, and scampered into the shade of the concealing forest. From there Alack sought various landmarks, learned where he is, and went to get the box he had stashed away.

Wearing only his torn pants and utility belt, he stank from the waters and two days of torture in the castle. His scent will lead the Zarbars to him. But for now, his moaning belly's needs are more important than his hygiene. Finding wild berries, melons and fruits, ate as he ran deeper into the woods. The vegetable matter had no effect on his raging appetite. His body craved the higher proteins and nutrients of animal meat.

Going down on his haunches, he yanked out the Bowie knife from the hidden holder within the belt, and sniffed the air, trying to get a scent.

All of his youthful hunting senses snapped on as subconscious talents during his days on Seminia took hold. If only Mushmoe was at his side, then the hunt would be complete.

Alack detected the right scent. Keen eyes darted to his left and spied a fuzzy animal nuzzling something from the ground. In a lightning leap, he dashed off to make his first kill in many years.

"Are you really going to slaughter that cute animal and eat it?" Danice's voice shattered the holographic image and the entire adventure scenario.

Alack, sitting on the floor in his black shorts, yanked off the intracranial headgear and flung it at the wall of her apartment. "DANICE!" His shout did not have any effect on her. "You ruined the mood…and killed the adventure!"

"After all these years we've known another you're still a wild best inside those shorts, Troyus." She removed her interfacing goggles and took a filled glass. "How long will it take for civilization to tame the savage hordes of Seminia? How long?"

Alack leaped to his socked feet and paced. His hair flailed as he pumped in a circle. "That was such a great challenge! I was winning!"

"It's not in your gut, Alack but in your mind…"

"I must be crazy to let you watch!"

She exhaled, long and frustrated. The flaxen blond hair was pulled back in a ring affair. The blue eyes sparkled with a touch of pity, her pretty face clear and intense. "Look at me. I don't need that wild stuff to have fun." She sipped a drink. "Just one of these, and I'm flying without that head shit."

"You're not Seminian with a raging beast within." He bent down and collected the pieces of the toy she bought him for his birthday.

She studied with impatience his firm athletic rump.

"Now I'll never know what happened…" He took the electronic and plastic pieces and disposed of them in the E-Waste bin.

She watched the perfectly muscular legs, heavy calves, the short shorts, and the powerful thighs tapering to a small waistline. Alack's small love handles and the spectacular upper body expansion to sturdy pectorals and broad shoulders, his latissimus dorsi and back muscles almost unreal in their size and girth. That thick neck held the peak of youth. Long bouncy blackish brown hair, thick auburn eyebrows, two big brown eyes with an intense sparkle, a face between the hardness of a man and the innocence of a boy, are all his assets in one 158 Illo (under 7 feet) package of raw Seminian humanity.

He caught her studying every muscle and movement. He knew exactly where her mind was. Puffing up his chest with a beasty snapping and popping of ribs and sinew broke a crafty smile. "You like? Life is here to be experienced."

"Yes…it thrills me when you do that in those shorts…"

"Gets your hormones banging and jumping?" He popped a bulging bicep.

"More like a dam breaking with cresting waves of destruction."

Alack made a muscleman pose, further pumping his exploding upper torso. "How about this…I've seen the professionals do this also."

"I'm so inflamed that a Tri-R squad must put out the fire."

He suddenly deflated himself and took a humble stance. "Well…forget it, you can't have it. So stay with your fantasies."

"Single mindlessness is a virtue of fools…" Danice tossed her empty glass at him. "You're worse than a Misk-a-dri teasing its captive before devouring it."

Alack caught the glass before it fell and broke. "Stop using my sayings, and when do we eat, I'm famished!"

"I think your still on that journey through the woods, Alack. Why don't we watch 'Journey Unknown', now that's excitement?"

"I know that show and Grewel Growlon is a phony."

"He's very interesting and you should read his books, you like that stuff." She made herself another drink. "I would think your last assignment, the Munshine Affair would teach you that."

"Good fortune will elevate even the petty minds. My friend Meander calls it 'journey unnecessary' and denounces him as a charlatan, a deceiver of the public to earn a fast credit, a sensationalist who…"

"He gives archaeological lectures at the biggest universities."

"And gets the biggest royalties for bringing in the crowds…" Alack found several bags of snack foods and began devouring them whole.

"Why does Mister Astrikon hate him?"

"It's not a question of hate, Danice but of exploitation of the ignorant mind." Alack got hold of more party foods and sat down on the living room carpet, munching away. "Example…" gulp, "a few years ago he claimed to find a Krillian ruin. He did a whole show on that…" gulp and munches, "a show that went nowhere and proved nothing."

"I saw that one, it was terrific."

"Two large stones had fallen upon another to form an arch. It was examined by experts and found to be natural," more gulps and louder munching noises. "He spent more time wearing fancy garments and shopping and eating at strange places. Then there was the Lost Stools of Citian, along the Reton Coast. He claimed the diamond shaped stones are the stairway of a lost temple to an undiscovered civilization. Soon after a group of investors built a series of hotels and vacation resorts capitalizing on the stools and old buildings around, and Valen Velamon, the Curator of Norume, discovered they are false."

"So, there's another one?"

Alack ignored her remark. "He analyzed the magnetic lines of force ingrained in the stone stools. If they were placed there by ancient hands the lines would be haphazard. But, they are all uniform. This means it's a natural magma flow that crystallized in a slow natural manner." Finishing his inhale of junk foods, Alack stood in a defiant manner, "the ancient ruins were found to be false, but your prized fellow received a hefty payoff to authenticate the site."

"You can be so annoying."

"How he got his own show is a mystery."

"Not to me..."

"He had to go to bed with the producer's daughter, lust is better than love."

"Alack! That's not nice..."

The doorbell chimed.

Danice went to open it but Alack stopped her. "You should check the exterior monitor."

She paused, making a silly grin, "afraid it's Growlon himself? I already know." She unlocked the door, opening it.

A cute little girl in a lavender blouse and pants suit with a business satchel tucked under her arm, a round baby face holding bright green eyes, topped off by a neat flock of curly auburn hair on the light side. Her lips broke a white, enchanting smile. "Danice! I finally meet you."

"Caroli, the 'board surfer' Muadon, come in." Danice closed the door behind her but did not lock it. This pretty intruder is welcome but will not stay long, Danice knows her habits.

"I was in the city shopping and…who's this?" The encounter happened so quickly that Alack had little time to get his moth-eaten robe on. "I like what I see. Is he fore sale or just the Super? If he is, the plumbing needs work." Her giggle filled the room like a lilac breeze.

"Neither. Sit and I'll make you a Tamaraw…you still drink them?"

"Oh yes, my stellar drink these days…" She eyed Alack's perfect round rump as he dashed from the room to get some clothes on. "Is he your new conquest?" She saw the mess on the floor. "Your taste in guys has improved." She took the foamy yellow concoction with a cherry on top. "The others lived in a sterile environment, this one's a real Bandalorian."

"He's just a friend that drops in occasionally…a good ear for the girl on the go."

"Looks like a fast-food platter takeout…with leftovers."

"So, you texted me that big things are happening?"

"Vastuum Studios called me yesterday…I'm so excited!" She started to choke on the lather of the drink. "They want me for a job audition!"

"This is wonderful!" Danice took Caroli's soft hands. "I'm so glad for you."

"They saw my stage video when it went live, and that's that!"

"Does your agent know?"

"I got rid of that phony years ago…he did nothing for me, a real pig of a Venderian, since I've been blowing my own horn and it finally happened!" Both hugged in a slushy manner. "You're the first to know."

"I'm really glad for you…you will stay in touch when you're up there with the cosmic crowd?"

Caroli downed the drink and stood grabbing her pouch. "Of course, friends are thicker than stellar dust…got to go…just wanted you to be the first, and YOU in the closet, glad to see you and your shorts, Good Looking and hunting."

Danice escorted her to the door. They kissed, Caroli left, Danice closed the door locking it. "You can come out Alack, its safe, she's gone."

"What was that all about?" He stood in his field clothes, white rubbery walking shoes, socks, black pants, thick belt and white plain short sleeved polo shirt on the tight side. "Your snacks had no effect…" He pounded his thin muscular abdomen. "And she only made it worse."

"Just a stellar-net friend, we talk when we need another, she's so sweet." Danice looked him over, made a frustrated sigh. "Don't you ever change your routine?"

"This is me Danice, like it or leave it," Alack grabbed his Calcomp stringing it over a broad shoulder. That signified he is done, ready to leave with or without her.

"If I didn't like it, I would have left it long ago. You don't want to eat in?"

"I want to try that Navatta eatery down the street, they just opened and I heard from other agents that the portions are very large."

"Are those agents still with the living? I'll join you; my day is still new."

Between assignments, Alack is very busy.

Sometimes a week (eight Amazian days) will pass before a call comes in from T.A. on a new 'Affair' he is asked for. Other instances it could be two weeks before his Boss orders him to appear. This is one such moment in his life he has lots of free time. The patrolling of the lands around for the Natural Park Reserve is an early morning two hour excursion on his scooter. Afterwards, doing little jobs around the Ranch house along Kensington Bay sucked away some of the boredom. Repair work added to other moments as he filled every second with something to do. Even taking a few trips to archeological digs in the area invited by his friend Meander, to help and study on the antiquities of the ancient Norumians. Other moments are a time of leisure and relaxation on the beach or in the surf.

It is during such an event of catching up on his reading that the house AI notified him of someone who just landed. The home Artificial Intelligence identified the Vehicle Code of the Zo, so when he opened the door, he knew exactly the person's name and what to say.

"She's dead!" Cried Danice as her mass of flaxen blond hair and wet face fell upon him. "Those bastards did it!" She almost knocked him over in her sobbing tantrums. "They made promises and never kept them…" A tidal wave of tears and remorse flattened Alack's resolve to resist. "She's gone!"

Closing the door Alack carefully guided her to the living room couch and gently placed her on the hard cushions. As she sobbed, hiding her strained face in a pillow Alack activated the BarBot and made her favorite drink. He returned with hers and a glass of DeMassie for himself. "Drink this Danice…" She grabbed his downing it in one gulp then took her own.  Looking for some strength until the wine took over made eye contact.  "Feeling better?"  He joined her on the couch.

"I got this in my E-Mail that Caroli…died in a freak accident…" A second explosive burst of wailing.  She fell onto Alack's shoulder spilling some of her drink.  "She was so innocent and sweet…so full of life and…and expectations…"  Calming down Danice fell back and sipped the remaining drops.  "How could you possibly know…?"  The pillow became a comforter.

Alack made her another.  "The past is always full of shadows, Danice."

"Oh!  Why did I even come here?"

"Because you must think something of me, friends give you an interest in life."

She suddenly paused, clinging to the Seminian rock she needs. "Try another…"

"That which is gone is precious?"

She exploded in a final wave of tears and laminations.  The pillow became a sounding board.

Alack gave her a strong hug, draining her of some emotions, then fell back on the couch holding her glass.  "Had enough?"  Eventually the tears turned into sniffles and those into quiet sipping of her drink. "Now, who is Caroli?"

Danice's sorry expression turned into rage.  "You muscle headed idiot…she's is…or was my friend from designer school."  She smacked him with the pillow.  "You met her last week at my place when you were in your underwear on my floor!  She's studying to be an actress and got employment at Vastuum Studios as a director's apprentice, don't you recall?"

Alack paused as his handsome face made a puckering. "Was she the one who…"

"Yes Alack, she's the one who ignored you and you hid in my bedroom."

"Now I remember, she was very focused and…" Danice swung the pillow at him. "I'm glad you're coming around, Danice."

"Again, I wonder why I came to you."

"As I said, friends give you an interest in life, or living."

She downed the drink in one swallow then held it out. "More! This gives me an interest in living. This has been a terrible day!"

Alack went back to the automated bar and returned with her drink. "Tell me more about Caroli?"

"Where do I start…we were friends at designer school, we went out together, partied together, dated together and we went our separate ways but stayed in touch, once a week e-posts you know, then she tells me something wonderful has happened and presto! She's at my door looking at you in your underwear…"

"Black exercise shorts, Danice."

"Regardless, very revealing…that's it…except for this…" Danice yanked out a hardcopy letter from her suit blouse combo and tossed it at him. "Read! Even a muscle can think!"

Alack studied it for a second. "This is a standard studio form letter, Danice," another pillow wacked him in the head.

"I didn't come out here for you to tell me what I already know!" She hit him again, hair flailing.

"Stop hitting me with things!" He waved the printed document like it was a surrender flag. "What more can I say?"

"You heartless Massolite!" She snatched it stuffing it away. "They killed her because she refused to be a plaything for their sex egos."

"How do you know that, Danice? That's a serious charge. Did she send you a final e-post saying that?"

"And if she did, what are YOU going to do about it?" She seized the same pillow but held back.

"I can open my own investigation, I'm Special Services…"

"Then read this, Servi Man." She tossed a small warped bundle of printed e-posts at him. "And I still like to throw things at your pretty face, Alack, you have so many muscles you can't be hurt, so don't ever think I can keep on trying!"


"When are you going to buy a newer Zo than continue to use this old rusty bucket?" complained Danice as she sat next to Alack. His restored Astra Mar Delux Z 25, built in 2010 by Reton Rockets, still had a musty, lived in odor. Ancient by modern standards, the entire interior has a fifty-year-old style that is an eyesore to her more up to date custom designs.

"This machine may not be to your pretty codes in office furniture, Danice, but it's me and I like it the way it is…and you are safer in this machine than in the newer models." Alack exhaled switching to autopilot pushing the half wheel aside. "We're at a safe altitude, now we must talk."

"What's to talk about? She's dead! They killed her."

"Before we land at Vastuum studios we must have a plan."

Alack opened his Calcomp bringing up the scanned hardcopy documents. "I read these, and despite the boring subject matter there is a progression of hints, getting more serious, to the last few texts are becoming alarming. Seems some dispute between her and her boss and a guy named Merril Edon, definitely some criminal thing going about at Vastuum that warrants an immediate investigation…"

"Thank you, Mister Alack Troyus!"

"We just can't drop in and start throwing accusations without evidence. The local Service Prefect will support the studio heads and kick us in the posterior."

"Say 'ass', it's better direct grammar."

"What we'll do we'll be as tourists, we'll take the regular tour, I'll slip away and go to her place of residency. I've done some research on the studio complex where she worked and they all live in an apartment complex on the studio grounds. I'll go there and get more evidence from her friends. They should have her personal items in storage. If they do, you can act as her family agent and retrieve them."

"She had no family. I was the closest thing to it."

"The more you do the social work upfront. Don't be afraid to use the power of attorney certificates if they give you a problem. If you seem weak, you'll get pushed around."

"In her last post, she felt someone was in her room late at night." A sniffle came after Danice's last word. "She was so innocent…"

"That feeling may have been conveyed to her friends. That's why you must gather them together in one group for questioning. But don't be direct, use the indirect method I taught you."

"How about a hanging party?"

"Let's find solid evidence first, Danice.  We worked together in the Florentine Affair, we can do better here."

They landed at a decent hotel in Batter City along the Galip Coast of the Newlon Sea.  Fifty Sectals (39 miles) inland, Caso Vastuum made his mark one hundred and fifteen years ago when he founded Vastuum Studios.  In the late Pre-Evil Times, shortly before the Unapiterian Conquest, the UAR Nation entertainment moguls experimented with celluloid and silver nitrate extracts to make motion picture film.  After the Conquest of the 1530's UC, the Unapiterians introduced an analogue video tape medium and later on a wire digital audio/video technology.  After the Amazian Revolt in the 1830's UC a digital magnetic tape medium was developed and eventually blossomed into digital computer recording systems of over one hundred bits per second.  By the time of Zaterite's reign in the 1928's UC a full entertainment industry provided the public with movies, plays, documentaries and musical shows for the domestic market and those homes who could afford the first televisor (TV) sets.

At one time all entertainment was provided by radio boxes and the theater districts in every major city on Amazia.  But an entrepreneurial producer of plays from Newlon City in the 1930's UC bought up four dying film studios.  He sold the assets of three and kept the Brandon Studios outside of Batter City renaming them Vastuum Studios.  When the powerful families who controlled the entertainment industry saw this upstart, they blocked his access to famous actors and actresses of those times.  But Caso Vastuum told his investors, "I don't care what they do.  I will make stars from the talented unknowns!"  And within twenty-five years he made Vastuum into a giant of the entertainment industry of Amazia.  He squashed and pulverized all those who opposed him with the finest productions of the times, adding high profits and great culture.

Caso died in 2031 UC and his son, Exter took over.  He upgraded all the audio and video equipment, going into the electronic digital medium producing films and shows far beyond Amazia and her new acquisitions.  As the Imperium expanded so did Vastuum Studios promoted the culture and heritage of the Amazian Race.  By the ascension of Civeron in 2041 UC Vastuum Studios owned entire worlds as lots for its productions.  Exter boasted their sets are real, breathing, natural sets, not fake photonic cutouts of the digital quantum mediums.  Under his control, Vastuum Studios became famous for gigantic epics with sweeping panoramas filled with thousands of extras.  It is said he made and broke movie stars and directors who dared to complain about his autocratic studio rule.  But everyone paid to see his films, shows, and productions, credits flowed, employment high making everyone happy.

Exter's son, Orben tried his hand at direction but screwed things up.  He had the bad habit of walking on a set, seeing something he did not like, fire the contracted director, and taking over the production himself.  Pampered, no one complained to the father until he tried it with Sara Klaron, Vastuum's biggest sex symbol since the Madame Maryvon Series.  She marched into Exter's office and told him off.  After that, Orben found himself at a desk, signing stagehand vouchers.  But, by the time he took over the studio system, Sara Klaron was gone and his ego tamed.  Orben took Vastuum Studios further by enhancing production using digital photonics, breaking away from the cheaper older video and audio mediums. This enabled cosmic broadcasting and took to the stars by selling entertainment packages to the military and even opened up various Alien studios on non-humanoid worlds. Vast studio sets that went unused, he organized theme park and family vacation tours around them. Some say he can beat the Lizyonites in their own game and squeeze credits from a worthless konderite asteroid.

His son, Motif, invested in the theme park ventures, adding to the overall profits. He went further and sponsored key electronic industries that set up home entertainment systems with cinema sound and wall sized hanging picture screens. Theater chains complained this would cause a severe drop off in box office profits, so Motif upgraded all of Vastuum's cinemas to make the ticket buyer be engulfed by the presentation on a full sensual scale. His endeavors in the public and commercial markets earned him several prestigious awards from industry moguls. Even the giant Pulta and Tusla space liners now had their own cinemas, making the spatial journey a delightful one.

"These are the original studio buildings from the Brandon Productions," shouted the Tour Guide as she stood at the front of the long outdoor Zo tram. Forty people of various ages and colors listened as heads turned to the neo-classical domed structure. "The first of Vastuum's films were made here, and when the Studio became a major player in the entertainment circuit, other buildings were built with more modern facilities for advanced technological productions. This structure is preserved and holds the balance of our tour, so kindly follow me." The tram stopped at a front door next to an immense pillared dome of sandalwood shingles.

The foyer, full of trophies, film awards, citations from three

Emperors, and many other memorabilia, had the four autocrats of Vastuum Studios on the walls in large dominating 3-D pictures that moved as you changed your perspective of sight. The Tour Guide briefly talked about each, praising and explaining their funny habits and charitable contributions. "When in 1979 the Tectonic Fracture damaged Newlon City Caso and Orben Vastuum held fundraisers and for every one Retallite paid at the box office went to rebuild parts of the city." The crowd followed her down the hall cluttered with awards of all shapes and sizes, including 'things' of Alien designs.

They entered into a cavernous interior of sets from the Studio's most famous film productions. One gigantic statue with moving limbs caught Danice's attention. "Look! It's Sara Klaron…my mother and her friends worshipped her…"

The immense image, with pearly light tan skin, pointed features twisted into the absurd, curving eyebrows bent down, a pair of heavy lips held a ridiculous ornate sweet stick at an obtuse angle of female defiance, the blondish grey hair sparkled with a shiny resonance under the cocked tam-o-shanter of dull blue. Her limbs are long, sharp and the breasts very firm, an enchanting image from an era long since glamorized.

"This is the Sara Klaron exhibit from her most famous film 'Queen of the Flaming World'. She is wearing the gown from her first film, 'Maur Amoura', the Island of Love in Delorian. These other sets are her with Yaullen Di from 'Stellar Stand', 'Lord of the Stars' and 'A Pirate's Affair'. She had her third husband star with her in 'Tyrant of Scalus'…"

"That's a Seminian…" mumbled Alack seeing both animated

figures on a veranda with two setting suns, "I've read about him, he was an outcast and died in poverty…"

Someone 'shhhed' him as the Tour Guide explained each set.

"Here she is in 'Master's Mistress', directed by Yart Zinar, who took the tragedy romance film into legendary status for Vastuum Studios." The tour rounded a corner to an elegant old world sitting room with antiques and a dozen live action mannequins. "Sara Klaron's mother, seen in this crime scene from the detective series 'Madame Maryvon' acted with her in the parlor interrogation, the dainty teenage girl on the left is Sara Klaron at twelve." They came to a set with no one on it.

Alack opened his Calcomp strung over his broad shoulder behind Danice and made a sensor scan. "Danice…these designs and flats are all artificial…holographic…"

More 'Shhes' from those behind him.

"This is the never made film 'Lady of Dalos', Sara Klaron perished aboard the Ethannec disaster in 2035 one million light years from Rominia." A gasp and hush swept the crowd. "The film 'Wake of the Stellar Queen', from the historical novel by E. Velon which was about her death, the rights were bought by Orben Vastuum so it could never be made into a film. He never forgave her for going into his father's office, resulting to his demotion. An illegal production of the book was made by our rivals, which was condemned as false, and there's no truth in the scenes where she seduced the Captain of the Ethannec, leading to the loss of that spatial liner."

"I've seen that movie," mumbled Alack to Danice, "but I don't recall anything like that…"

Another 'shhh!' made Danice give him a sorrowful look.

"If you follow me, we will now go to the Monts Cylin exhibit, Vastuum's greatest dramatic director.  He made more stars than all our rival studios combined…"

When the tour group entered a set with massive pillars and heavy stone work, Alack stepped quietly out of line and hung in the shadows waiting for the right moment. Finally, alone, found a rear exit door and left the domed structure.  Getting his bearings from the studio guide brochure made his way to the resident building area.

"You there!" shouted a Security Guard in a drab grey uniform. "You're going the wrong way, follow me."  Alack, not wanting to cause attention, obeyed meekly.  They ended up in a room with two dozen other hefty looking guys, bright lights against a castle in the mountain's diorama.  A Starflex multi lens camera sat on a remote stand with three seats holding the posteriors of others.  Several well-dressed people with fancy Calcomps stood off behind the camera talking in wild hand gestures.  "I found one of your guys wandering outside," stated the Security Guard pushing Alack into the lineup.  "Stand here."  And the Guard left, giving the three fellows a wink gesturing to his badge number.

Alack took his place at the end of the lineup looking dumb, 'when in Norume do as they do.' He thought.

"Stop the ship!  Stop everything!  That's the man I want!"  A funny, chubby faced Amazian in a massive wraparound scarf affair with three others in tow approached Alack.  "He's perfect!  Dismiss the others…"  The Fellow started to study Alack up and down with an optical sensor attached to his left eye.

Alack stood somewhat at attention.

From his rubbery walking shoes, up his black pants revealing his muscular legs and thighs, to the disguised utility belt around his thin waist, rising to the white short sleeved polo shirt on the tight side, finalizing to the handsome face, big brown eyes, heavy lips and long well-groomed auburn hair hanging down to a slight curl, the desirable features of a young humanoid with advancing chiseled outlines.

"Call the talent agency, I'll take a dozen!"

"There's great potential here," said a Female with various hanging measuring devices on her pants suit combo. "Yes, great potential. We can use the Folton Method on the forehead, put the spike in there, the hair can be braided to hang as deadlocks with bowties, a few piercings along the cheeks and nose…" She walked around Alack eyeing his spectacular physique, "according to the historical depictions he was covered in tattoos of his sexual exploits, on a body like that we have plenty of room!"

"I knew the right one would come along." The chubby Fellow smiled up at Alack. "You've got the part, let me see your SAK card?" Alack frowned down at him.

"Uh…I don't have that, Sir…"

"What!" All the others crowded around him; one guy activated a list on his Calcomp. "Where did you come from?"

"The tour group, Sir…I got lost…"

"He's not on the agency's list, Mister Qrewon."

The chubby Fellow slumped, "and I thought this would be easy…do you want to be an actor? Are you camera shy? I can arrange a screen test? Just name your price?"

"Thank you, Sir, but no!"

The slightly obese Fellow exhaled in frustration, stepped away as the group followed him. "Round up those guys and get them back in here, we'll take this from the top!"

Alack is escorted off the lot and abandoned. He went back to his original course and found the tenant building. Tucked away in a secluded park area with picnic benches, a gazebo, small pond with fountains, and several shady cooking grills, is a fine place to live and work. The residency is several stories high in creamy bricks with lots of windows and fancy stone work along the seams. A wide foyer, no security guards but a receptionist, greeted Alack as he stepped in.

Telling her he represents the estate of Caroli Maudon asked about her private possessions.

The elderly Lady hesitated, read some text messages on her computer screen then gave her condolences. Leading Alack to a storage room, he studied the layout, where the exits are and elevators. She opened a closet and gave Alack a large plastic box, telling him all her stuff is in here. "She wasn't here that long to accumulate much."

Thanking her Alack took the box and found Danice waiting for him in front of the main studio building; the tour was done.

They returned to their hotel to sort thru Caroli's items. "Not much here," mumbled Alack checking photos and some e-books from her student days.

"How did you get this?"

"My good looks."

"She always traveled light. Not one for stockpiling junk."

Alack moved away, seeking another diversion. He hotwired his

Calcomp into the Hotel's network link and accessed the Batter City's Zoning Office. Using his secret entry codes found the design plans for the residency building. Taking a moment to study the layout, he made a final decision and downloaded them onto his hard drive, then carefully backed out. "What room was she in?"

"She took a third-floor suite…on the south side…room 315, why?"

"I'm going back there tonight." Alack brought up the design specs on his Calcomp and found her room. "Do you know if it's occupied?"

"Why don't you access the front desk, Octor's apps can do anything."

"I tried, that system is totally independent." A loud gurgling sound filled the room with a bombastic grunt of inner juices. Alack stood and slapped his stomach muscles under his shirt. "Let's eat! I'm ravenous!"

"When the belly speaks, the beast must jump." She giggled, finding his abnormal habits amusing. "You can order room service or we can try out that deli across the street. Big decision, Troyus?"

"The Deli. I have no idea if room service will give me enough."

She watched that handsome face inhale two meat hoagies, with cheese bread pieces and washed it all down with a lemon tonic drink. Alack slumped in the chair digesting, eyes closed, and breathing through his mouth. She is use to his freakish intake of proteins and nutrients, like a cavalry charge. She knows he has no toleration for hunger, no fatty tissues to take up the slack. Alack is all powerful muscle, tensile sinew and terrible strength. She has seen him in action, a super physical machine that can be terrifying to the enemy and lifesaving to those he marks as a friend.

After a loud burp, he came alive.

"What do we do next?" asked Danice in a whisper.

"It all started here…" he began with another loud, pleasing burp.

"Two? You're bad manners?"

"The Tasshonevic (Toshivic) Revolution, Danice. Don't you know your Amazian history?" He never let her answer. "The cry was 'from Moliny to Batter'. Batter City in those days was named Maker, the capital of the Marhous Kingdom. The Intercontinental War of the 1350's ended with the Pre-Evil Nation UAR as overall victor and seized all the lands…"

"That was 1731, what does this have to do with that?"

"Allow me to set the history, please!" A long exhale and Alack continued. "On a warm night Edward Constonline and Hans Rezeint, with a band of brave and daring young men, seized the Unapiterian missile cruiser Fabernar from the naval base at Moliny, went up the Galip coast to Maker and attacked the 6th Infantry Division Arsenal outside of Maker City. They used the code name 'Battle' to alert the rebel forces under Naponte when to attack the fort. Somehow the code was sent as 'Batter' and that's how this city got its name. The Amazians began their revolt against Lussontwin the 'enslaver' Unapiterian general. As I said, it all began here, Danice."

"I read someplace this city was called Helious by an ancient tribe."

"Yes, the Tobotus, who fought the Norumians and were defeated. The Norumians turned their lands into the province of

Caladon and Helious changed to Heshum. After the fall of Norume, the barbarian tribe of the Marhouse settled this area, do you want me to repeat myself?"

"No. Two burps are enough. I want to go back to the hotel and go through Caroli's stuff again."

"Okay, back to the Hotel…nap time…a tired mind knows no peace."

"Hopeless…"

Alack paused in his thoughts, a tiny piece of observation came up from his thick skull. "I need more research on that building, it doesn't look right…"

"You're going back there tonight, aren't you?" She almost collided into his rear when he stopped abruptly.

"Yes, that's very good, Danice, you know me to well." Both exited and crossed the Silorian (street).

"Let's focus on who killed Caroli rather than some funny blue prints. It had to be someone associated with who she worked for." They entered the Hotel lobby and took the elevator up. "Her boss was Marjer Herlon, assistant producer to Motif Vastuum himself. According to the brochures, there's seven Producers under Motif." They entered their room, Alack locking the door. "Each one has a young assistant like Caroli who does all the secretarial leg work. The whole operation is very lean and free of bureaucracy." Alack is removing his shoes, socks, pants and shirt, curling up on the hard rug of the floor. Danice gave Alack a swift kick in his posterior black shorts. "She claims they tried to seduce her!"

Alack squinted up at her. "It's my nap time…"

"That can wait. This is reality, Troyus! Not betty-bye."

Alack shot up like a flash. "No, it isn't, Danice." His massive chest bulging, he pounced at her. "This whole industry is a fantasy! A great big dream that has gone crazy and your sucked into it, manipulated, reformed, and recast, then spat out." She fell back from his emotional onslaught. "That Seminian, the plaything for Sara Klaron, broke all the taboos of my people, and when he found his life was nothing but an illusion with no substance, he, hung himself from a dumpster." Her back is to the wall, those handsome features, a clouding storm of anxiety. "Those sets are photonic particles, the glamour, the glitz, the fashions, the false hopes, and the devious ideals, all part of the illusion. The only thing that's real is the credits. What goes from your pocket into theirs, that's the reality here! Caroli died because she refused to be part of that charade. She refused to do the bidding of someone named Merril Edon and her boss, Herlon. The sexual part is only an effect of some greater stimulating crime!" He suddenly inhaled and exhaled, shaking himself, throwing off the tension and anxiety. "Now I need my rest to think so I can act." With that weird, unreal outburst, Alack flopped to the floor, curled up like a puppy, yanking a shabby sleeping cloth over his limbs, and fell into slumber.

Within seconds, the mass of muscles snored.

Danice did not move. The force of his will glued her to the wall in the hotel room. When she got up enough courage to make herself a strong drink, she thought she saw her outline in the creamy tan of the plasterboard. So intense was Alack's burst of energy that it left her drained and weak. For a long time, she sat there thinking, reflecting, feeling her ego restore her power and self-drive. By the time Alack began to stir, she had cooked dinner and had another round for herself and for him.

The muscles unraveled, kicking the cover aside.

He started to stretch in a prone position. She became thrilled and excited within as she watched his shorts bulge and almost tear over his thighs. The arms went up. Clawing, grasping, the upper body tendons straining, ribs popping, pectorals ready to shred, and Alack's waist slimmer than she can imagine. He twisted, touching both toes. Then both palms came down to grasp the rug. Lifting himself up, into a straddle to a handstand, curled, and landed on his big feet. A gigantic inhale, yanked his left leg up high with his arm doing a 'Y' scale and then back to a resting stance.

He saw her delighted. "You like?"

"I like everything you do…and wear." She held up a glass of DeMassie wine.

Alack took it sitting next to her. "Thank you." His warmth is like a furnace, and his body odor is sweet and enticing. "Now touch me."

"Don't push it."

"But I want to, Danice. I'm real, I have substance, strength, and this." He pointed to the bulge in his black shorts. "Not that fantasy crap we saw today."

"Say what you think, Mister Reality, but you enjoyed the 'Etessian Love', and that's from Vastuum."

"Yes, I did, but that was more instructional, so I can deal with you." He gave her his weird smile with the ends of his lips up. "And I apologize for my outburst. You know me Danice, I prefer something realistic, raw, tangible, something I can solve and feel with my mind and put my fist through…then again…I was tired…"

"Accepted, in both categories, Sweet Alack, dinner awaits."

"The best of men fears nothing, eat on!"


That evening, Alack stripped down to his black shorts and tightened his utility belt around his slim waistline.  Wrapping a pair of elastic gloves over his hands and feet, which will prevent any prints or DNA seepage, Alack inhaled and exhaled, clearing his mind for the ordeal.  Feeling fit and renewed after eating everything she had prepared, went out late into the night.  Taking the Zo car, Alack turned on the stealth field so their security could not detect and landed near the tenant building.  He did a quick ground scan to see if any sensors were around.  Finding no outer surveillance, a simple flipping twist of a jump and Alack's over the fence and in.  Staying in the shadows, the padded foot Giant made it to the resident building within minutes.  Using trees, benches and fountains as blinds, made his way to the rear.  Knowing the design found a darkened shadow niche between the brick pilasters and climbed.  The way the brickwork is styled made it easy for him to ascend.  Like a great obscured spider crawled up and over the balustrade to the roof.  Finding the maintenance door, scanning for any hidden sensor alarm with his Mini-Comp on the belt, found none, twisted the locking mechanism off and entered.

Down the stairwell to the third floor, Alack opened the fire door and scanned for bio life signs.  Nothing registered and entered the carpeted hallway.  The night lamps are feeble so he made his way to Caroli's old room.  The snoring and light sleeping music told him everyone was tucked in for the night. Scanning for internal signs of an occupant and motion sensors, found nothing, and quietly twisted the knob until it snapped. The door creaked open, and Alack stepped in, closing behind him.

Putting on his night vision glasses, he finds the room is much smaller than he thought. A thick carpet his feet sunk into stifled any noise as he continued to scan. The room is unoccupied, no tenant has been brought in, and it looks like there has been no maid service yet. Feeling confident, Alack sought Caroli's DNA and other tidbits of evidence explaining her sudden death. His biometric scans detected her imprints in the carpet fibers, plus the shoe marks of the person who gathered her personal items. Caroli must have been barefooted during her last moments. Her DNA perspiration signature is faint but readable. Following her progress from the bedroom, then a startled shift of her feet position, another set of prints from someone with very heavy shoes, and where her body fell. By the minute distortions in the rug some struggle took place, even certain fibers are ripped and torn.

Alack traced the Intruder's prints to an empty wall.

The Murderer did not come in through the door.

Alack suddenly got an idea and paced counting the size of the room with his feet. Checking the tiny digital display from the Zoning Office this room is seventy-two Illos (3 feet) to short. Going back to the wall Alack reasoned there is a hidden passageway behind. Using a neutrino scan found a tight corridor beyond the plasterboard wall. His scan told him it is only one Illo (half an inch) thick as opposed to the other walls of greater thickness.

Making a fist Alack punched a hole. In one titanic surge yanked the hidden door out and onto the carpet. Deciding to go all the way, entered the concealed space.

It is a virtual maze of secret corridors. Stairs going up and down, every room has a hidden access door. In the clandestine corridor by each secret door is an audio/video setup controlled from a central location, anything said and viewed is imaged within the room, is known. Checking the recording device for Caroli's room found the memory data crystal removed. Whoever built this had a twisted sense of cloak and dagger dramas. Then again this is a movie lot with twisted fantasies and unreal expectations. But here, whoever conceived this espionage nightmare has direct access to anyone of the occupants. In the darkness, Alack's mind jumped about, recalling Caroli's anxieties about being watched, even to the point of paranoia. People living and working here are at the mercy of some sinister force not moral or ethical.

Danice must pry open their anxieties.

With that driving him, he followed the musty passageway, scanning for footprints in the dust. Finding many shoe variations recorded as much as he could discern. Eventually the whole clandestine maze was emptied out by a service entrance in the back by the recycling dumpster. Checking for faint imprints in the dirt found a recent pair before they ended in the grass. By the looks, they are pretty new, very large and heavy, around the time Caroli was killed.

Seeing enough, an idea exploded within. Alack headed back to his Zo car and the Hotel to contact the Special Customer Service Department of the Special Services.

In the morning, after a gigantic breakfast that made Danice sick to watch him, Alack dressed in formal suit clothes. Polished black shoes, grey straight pants, utility belt snuggly around his slim waistline, plain grey shirt with fluff around the neck and sleeves, a long grey waist coat with fancy trim but no outer pockets. His hair was meticulously styled, over his forehead, hanging down and tapering up at the neck in a slight curl. His face, between the softness of a boy and the chiseled features of a man, is determined and on a mission. Grabbing his Calcomp, Alack strung it over a broad shoulder.

"She's dead and you're dressed for a funeral!" sniffed Danice emotionally. She still held a fancy metallic bottle and was up all night sorting her items and suffering from the memorabilia. "We must do something!"

"I am…" and Alack left Danice to wallow in her repeating emotions.

He has an appointment with the Prefect of Batter City.

Deciding to introduce himself as Salus Sandavon, a relative of Caroli, to seek more information about her death, plus see if the Prefect is involved. Alack used his covert identity and accessed the Social Service Bulletins of the Prefect's department. On this social media websites for SSG people there are family shots, parties, and award ceremonies, all posted for the personnel to show. Alack found numerous shots of the Prefect with Marjer Herlon, Juballa Vastuum, Motif's son, a guy labeled Merril Edon and many other studios people, actors, and actresses at sexy parties and film galas.

If the Prefect is corrupt, he wants to sow the seeds of deception. He wants to create two people than one. In this situation, a duality tactic may work. He waited in the reception room. As he sat there thinking, he caught the numerous pictures on the walls of Prefect Ballyhon issuing citations, dedicating medals, attending fund raisers, and receiving civic awards. In all the pictures are members of the upper echelon of Vastuum Studios. A sudden shudder went through his body as the evidence seemed overwhelming. Like in the Praxis and Quenar Affairs, the SSG Captain was corrupted by big power and money. Is Ballyhon so cashiered?

Smart move, Troyus, 'inspiration creates action, flattery creates idleness', changing identities will be an advantage here, he reasoned.

"The Prefect will see you now, Citizen Sandavon from S. P. & P. Imports."

"Thank you." Alack went into the office of Ballyhon, more pictures and trophies with the Vastuum executive crowd.

"Yes, how can I help you…?" Alack showed him his citizen ID. "Yes, of course, Mr. Sandavon, I was told this is an emergency?" Both men sat. "Your secretary said it was of the utmost importance, Sir."

"My family just received the word that a relative, Caroli Muadon has died at Vastuum Studios where she was working. One of our sister-in-laws with her boyfriend has retrieved her personal effects, but not the body, is there a problem, Sir?"

"Oh yes, yes, I remember this tragedy, a shame, such a nice pretty girl. Didn't they give you the SSG Report? I'll have to speak with the head of studio security, he's so busy guarding the stars, I guess it slipped his mind." Ballyhon pressed a button on his wide desk. "Mrs Walliskon, the Caroli Muadon death at Vastuum, I need our SSG Report on her fatality." He glanced at Alack's handsome features. "What relationship is she to you Sir? I thought she had no living family, as per her employment form."

"I'm her Uncle Salus Sandle, before my name was Saturnized to Sandavon, for salesman purposes."

"I deplore that stupid, silly custom. It confuses our record keeping."

"The curse of Empire, Sir." grinned Alack agreeing with him.

A data crystal popped up from a slot on his desktop. "This is for you, Mr. Sandavon. I thought we issued this already. Is there anything else?"

"My Brother has the original, but we're not talking, a family matter Sir. I assume your death certificate is for tax purposes, and…uh, is the autopsy and corner's report included?"

"None was necessary…the fallen dolly crane was fatal, self-explanatory, Sir. Everything you need is in my report."

"Okay…" Alack stood, placing the glassy crystal in his pocket. "One last request, may I see the body so I can arrange transport to Newlon City. The services will be held there."

"Oh my, uh…didn't you know, she was cremated yesterday. We don't allow any cadavers, human or alien, to remain for no longer than two days tops. Safety concerns of health, sanitation, and religion, you know."

Alack frowned over this one. "Religion? What religion, she never made any reference to an active faith. I think she was an atheist."

"The cremation is Marhon Law, Sir, according to the Cyrenic Creed."

"Okay, but the crane, was it properly maintained?"

"It's all in my SSG Report, and your friend Danice Elzeron has the urn with other personal materials, so good day Mr. Sandavon."

Security Chief Darius Movallis stood in the apartment with another inspecting the broken plasterboard wall. The Superintendant made an estimate repair bill on this Calcomp as he conferred with the Studio contractor via the built-in portafon. Mumbling he would be back, left the room.

Prefect Ballyhon walked in and halted. "He did this?"

"As I said, our intruder has excellent physical abilities." Movallis held up a plastic bag with two broken door locking mechanisms. "Check this for biometrics, I want a full SSG report, Corey." Ballyhon took it accepting the harsh attitude of the Studio security head. "He came in from the roof, must have a hover Zo or scooter."

"Uh…have you heard anything about my script?"

"This isn't the time!"

"I worked hard on the history, how the 'magical sword' was used by Constonline and stolen by Admiral Naponte for his own selfish use. Great drama and patriotism here Darius, with all the elements of an epic, even a romance between Lussontwin's daughter and Rezeint. It's a dead ringer for a credit-making stellar hit!"

"You'll be the first to know when Herlon tells me. Now stay focused."

"He better! All the covering up I've done to save his ass, I should write a new script about his sex-charades, it might get banned by the Emperor himself."

Movallis bit his lip and gave the Prefect a cold hard stare. "If you do…"

"Forget it. I'm just tired of being a busboy for that Venderian."

"We're all busboys in this racket, well paid, and liking it."

"Okay, yes, back to the matter at hand. You think Sandavon did this?"

"Either him or the girl's boyfriend. Have you figured out who he is?"

"The boyfriend is Alack Troyus, a terrain Ranger out by the Colossus Reserve Park, who has connections with the SSG. He is the brother of Sandavon, and changed his name because of a family dispute, not for business reasons, as he told me."

"You haven't answered my question, did the boyfriend do this? He has the body and muscles of a weightlifter."

Ballyhon stood assured. "I think he did. We found no DNA or other prints, and Troyus has assisted the SSG in crime solving. He was involved in some big court case at the Capital a few years ago, pretty intense legal stuff from what I recall. He was in your tour group and retrieved the dead girl's items, so he knew of the dormitory's location."

Movallis scratched his neck in thought. "Then, in your opinion, who is the most serious threat here?"

"Terrain Rangers have unique talents, a salesman doesn't. I'll bank on the boyfriend. With a body like that, he can easily punch a hole in your wallboard or climb up the side of this structure, or descend in a gravimetric scooter using stealth. As I said, he has unique talents and training."

"Then, he knows the layout of this place and spying equipment." The Security Chief of Vastuum Studios took on a Napoleonic pose and paced. "I need to confer with Herlon and Juballa over this. If we botch it up it may explode into a serious scandal.  If handled rightly we can bury it so deep no one will find it.  This is unlike the others; they were easy to hide.  But Herlon acted too soon, he's listening way too much to that Venderian Edon, causing us to be sloppy.  Maybe this conference will knock some sense into his thick head."

"When you're with Herlon check on the status of my script," Cory Ballyhon broke a pleading grin.  "I want something better when I retire."


"Why didn't you tell me you got her funeral urn?"  Alack glared at the ceramic vase with wings and things prancing around the bowl.

"You just left, and the call came from the coroner's office, what could I do?"  Danice pleaded in a half rebuttal and half squeaky child's voice.  Caught in between, she made a cute girly face, fluttering her eyes to get sympathy.  "I've got to do more than morn over Caroli's death.  I have to talk to her friends!"

Alack, after changing into his salesman's clothes, exhaled, accepting the situation.  "I found the place they hang out on a certain evening, and we intend to go there now."

"They'll open up more to me than you."

"Okay Danice, but I'm going as Salus Sandavon from S. P. & P. Imports, not as Alack Troyus, you must call me Sal, and whatever I say you must agree.  In this scenario, Alack Troyus is my brother who I don't like…"

"Why?  Alack is a wonderful guy."

"Just agree!"

It is a small night club called Sprockettes that the workers of

Vastuum Studios in Batter City along the main drag, they went to. Entering at the evening hour, lung weed and other drugs filled the air, show time music bounced loudly off the walls. The decor is geared for film buffs. Pictures lined the stucco paneling of famous actors and actressess from Vastuum, none from the rival studios. A big portrait of Sara Klaron glared down on the cliental, painted in oils and crystallized sparkles on a velvet medium almost seemed alive without holographics. Protecting glass prevented the smoky atmosphere from clouding her sacred image. The bar is a half-circle with sturdy seats done in red Treout (horse) leather. It is here Alack and Danice plopped their posteriors amongst the seventy so occupants.

"That face can be riveting," mumbled Alack handing Danice her drink. "Lust is better than love."

"That wasn't nice, Salus. She was big in her day. My mother said she grew so big they couldn't make a digital screen large enough to satisfy her." The painting's eyes seemed to catch your attention, they moved when you moved. "They say she became impossible to please…"

"Don't look Danice, now I see why that Seminian fell under her spell."

"Okay Salus, I won't lose my cute demure, abandon family and friends and get aboard a space liner destined for destruction."

Alack found her enchanting. The murky light at the bar, reflecting off the vast array of bottles behind, added an eerie quality to her features. No makeup, a plain youthful face of natural oils and skin, is Danice's main attribute. "You're very pretty in your pants suit, Danice. Forget Sara Klaron, there's no competition here."

"That was nice…oh look!  At that table with the red heads…it's Grewel Growlon, that archeological guy you don't like."

Alack shifted his position asking for a menu from the Bartender but used his new angle to study his prey.  Making a mental note, mentioned to the Bartender is that Growlon?  The Bar Keep frowned, shucked his youthful head and mumbled something else.  He took Alack's order and went to the kitchen monitor to order the request.  Alack went back to Danice.  "Are you sure that's Growlon?  The Bartender says that's Merril Edon, the guy Caroli mentions in her posts, and who I've seen with the Prefect at many parties."

"You went to parties without asking me!"

"The social media Service Bulletins…" growled Alack.  "The past is full of shadows."

"Sometimes those shadows are all over your face.  I don't know who Edon is but I'm sure that's Growlon."

"Then he's going under a different name to avoid something."

"Like you Salus?  Your past is full of shadows.  I think it's time to work this room..."  Alack's order arrived, two big plates of finger foods and eating utensils.  "And you do your job."  She made a gesture at the food.  As Alack gorged himself on the Shelban Puffer platters, Danice carefully opened conversations with a female's face found in Caroli's posts, as a friend.  This led into other workers from the Studio who knew Caroli, and by the time she finished her mission returned to the bar.  Alack had three plates licked clean and gravy stains over his grey Nehru business shirt and an oily mess all over his mouth and hands.  "You're such a dugart (wild pig)!  All these years with ME and you still haven't learned proper eating hygiene?"

"The only time a guy from Seminia starts caring about hygiene is when he starts the marriage ritual, and you know I live to eat…" he mumbled, breaking a dirty child's grin.

"You live to make a mess." She grabbed a wet towel from the Bartender, who also witnessed the Young Man's lustful consumption. Danice began to wash him down like an infant in a stroller. "The Shelban platter is eaten with this spoon and tweezers utensil…"

"Oh! I was wondering what that was for…"

"Not with those big clumsy fingers, Salus. Too much pressure breaks the soft shell and you get the oily gravy all over, but some people need a lesson in etiquette."

"Why don't you teach me, Danice? Like tonight, after a romantic drink out on the balcony overlooking the city lights?"

She took her previous seat next to him as the Bartender pushed a drink at her. She ignored Alack's attempt to be sexy. "You're Sweet, are you full time here?"

Yes, Madam, but I'm studying to be a dramatic actor."

"How nice. You've got a pretty handsome face and lots of hair, like Salus. They approached him for a part but he turned them down. He's not into the glitz and pizzazz that goes with the job. He likes to buy and sell things that he can touch."

"But Madam…that is the job. Excuse me." And the Bartender stepped away to serve a customer.

"See how easy that was?" She held up a data crystal to Alack. "The conversations of a dozen people who knew Caroli, but not their names and addresses. There's some SSG at-a-boy, a 'boot beater' who is hungry for me and he can get a list of occupants at the dormitory so you can issue subpoenas for testimony in court." She made a sly grin, her red lips gently defining her superior talents, further driving a nail into his brain.

Alack took the data crystal after cleaning the grease from his hands. "Excellent… Where did you learn to do that?"

"From you stupid." She tossed her flaxen hair back in a defiant, uppity manner. "Someone had to save the day. There's more going on here than movie making."

"Yes, I can now see that, and get that name list, please?"

"We don't have visual holographics for sets…" shouted Marjer Herlon at the stunned novian on the desk monitor. "We have entire worlds that are sets. When you see a sun rising or a deep misty canyon or a blue ocean, they are real! Not a digital creation by our rivals, you read my words?" The young reporter did not have a moment to reply. "So, if one of our actor's steps in dog shit its real, got that?" The young Novian made a reply, more of an apology, if he wants a story. "Good boy. If you want an interview, I'll be dining alone this evening at Baldars at the corner of Toshivic and Masteron Way. Be there at zero two hundred and bring yourself only, plus money, you're earning this if you like it or not." He closed the connection, the screen going dark and slowly slipping back into his wide curving desk. Turning his gruff, ugly wrinkled face at the two guys in his office, grumbled, "This better be important."

"It's the Caroli Maudon mess…" the Security Chief went right to the point. "Things are turning ugly, Marjer. We have her friend and a family member investigating her death. Eventually, they'll learn the truth of how and why she died."

"It's all his fault!" Herlon jabbed a head jerk at the other Fellow. "If she didn't discover those buried bodies were real, you won't be bothering me. I've told you Edon, stay away from the hired help. Your married, damn it!" Herlon swung his automatic chair around. It buzzed away from the curving side of his desk to face them both, "Seems there's a short supply of chastity around here." The leg braces came to life and he stood, towering over them like some terrible giant on a rampage. The face twisting in a menacing manner, "led'em all into the desert and bury them, like those old sets from the days of Brandon Studios." Herlon stopped, swung around facing Merril Edon, who quietly studied his boss. "Be dramatic about it…some type of sinkhole that has no bottom!"

"This isn't a film plot, Marjer," began the Security Chief. "These people can cause us all an embarrassing situation if they get the SSG involved…"

"Then squash it! Terminate the evidence. Who's that Prefect again?"

"Uh…Bellyhon…"

"What will make him cross the line?"

"He…uh, he has a film script he's written and submitted…"

"Is that the piece of Treout trash from the battle of Batter City?"

"Yes! Buy that script and make a promise, and he'll do anything you ask."

"I don't make promises," Herlon seemed to frown, making a decision, "but if it will get him to do your bidding, I'll buy it and file it away so whoever sits behind that desk after I'm gone can keep the lie going." He slammed his fist into his palm, the cracking clap made both jumps. "Get that bastard and get rid of those people, and now!" Herlon kicked the carpet, the massive foot taking some fibers with it, "we have a billion credit brain child in the making, and nothing will stop the wheels from grinding it out. When Sylas Brandon made his film a hundred and fifty years ago and buried those sets, he covered Silentium bullion for us to exploit." Herlon stamped about in a tirade, both fellows fell back when their boss is on a cinematic roll.

"I've got a dozen Brilliantines from the Universities working with me Herlon, we'll make a fortune for Motif and the studio," added Merril Edon smiling broadly.

"Right! No one remembers the Sands of Sasha. The print is gone and the fire destroyed all production stills and notes. All personnel are long dead and maybe some film buff dying of dementia might recall, let him rave and be called mad by the critics who'll be praising our archeological theme park resort!" Herlon made two fists grasping the air like some villain from the taped thrillers. "We'll have the biggest stellar stars Motiff can muster, a gigantic entertainment center for celebrities of shapes and weird sizes, a sweeping panorama of the desert with pools, exotic animals from the far corners of the Imperium, the tastiest restaurants Juballa can imagine, fine hotel rooms, the best Sporadium under the Ring!" So puffed up with his ambition, Marjer Herlon started yelling for his secretary. "The world is mine to devour and taste!" The others laughed over the famous line of Sara Klaron.

But they did not realize Herlon-was dead serious.

"They told me weird stories of young girls hired as production assistants for the five studio heads, Alack." Danice explained as they sat under a comfortable canopy at a street café in Batter City. "After a few weeks they suddenly changed."

"How did they change?" asked Alack dressed as the salesman Sandavon. He inserted a limited recording device into his shirt collar, making various adjustments for audio-only. "I'm dying to try this."

She ignored him, "Lots of anxieties at first, dreams, voices, whispering like someone was watching you as you slept, or exercised or showered in the privacy of your room. Some of the girls say they saw shadows on the walls, heard footsteps in the living room and even doors opening and closing. After a month they all became paranoid and began to lock themselves in their bedrooms…"

"Some of those secret corridors entered into their sleeping quarters."

"It gets worse. One night one of the secretaries found a guy in her closet smelling her clothes. Then another said she woke up, startled by heavy breathing, and there was this large man staring down at her, drooling. When she finished screaming, he was gone."

"Did they all file complaints?"

"Yes. But nothing came of it. The security guy…"

"That's Darius Movallis."

"He did nothing blaming it on hallucinations caused by the pleasure drugs they were taking after working hours. Caroli never took drugs and she began to have the same anxiety attacks." Danice finally exhaled, blowing her wad of words.

"Did they talk to the Service Prefect?"

"Yes again. A secret group went to see him to file a complaint but he told them the place was haunted. Several people died a violent death and their mental anguish energy was still in the walls and ceilings. What cinematic bullshit story is that?"

"It makes for higher drama, Danice." Alack sipped his drink. "Death is a simple business. What happened to that secret group?"

"Uh, they were re-assigned…off world to another production studio. Caroli's friends think they got promotions…never seen or heard of again."

"Did you get the full list of names?"

"A piece of pie, Sweet Alack. Not a bad fellow, we had a good time. Even I can make promises I won't keep."

Alack changed the subject quickly. "Any more details on how she died? That crane accident out on the film set?"

"Yes, a third time. When I got her urn I asked the Prefect for a maintenance report on the accident, and he promised to get back to me. That was two days ago, nothing since."

At that moment, several shadows fell upon them at the secluded table.

Prefect Bellyhon and Security Chief Movallis introduced themselves in a polite manner. "We're glad we found you," Grinned Movallis in a sinister way.

"Willingly, of course, Miss Elzeron, and I owe you an apology for the delay."

"The accident of Caroli Maudon, we want to take you to where it happened and show in detail how the tragedy unfolded," again that sinister grin.

"It should only take an hour of your time, and you, Citizen Sandavon, you may join us as a second party of the family." Bellyhon extended his palm to a waiting Zo vehicle with the studio's logo on the door.

Wondering why it is not a SSG car, Alack sent his mind out touching the two. The returning impressions are so devious that the hairs at the nape of his neck almost tingled, signaling great danger. As Danice got up Alack reached into the folds of his pompous suit and opened the holster flap of his Anti-D pistol on his concealed utility belt. Feeling this will solve certain issues and bring this to a conclusion, decided to allow the trip. Knowing Danice is in great danger, this is not the first time they have shared in a criminal action, and he has always been there to safeguard her. Alack also knew they think he is just an overly large salesman without any training to resist, and they think whatever they are going to do will be easy. 'This will be a knife in soft cheese,' Chuckled Alack to himself.

They got into the four-seater and went aerial once they were beyond the city's perimeter.

Alack studied every landmark as they headed out over farmland, suburbs, small industrial parks and to a section of finger deserts. This area, one hundred Sectals (79 miles) from Batter City inland, is the Sasha Finger Waste, the very beginning of the vast Catslind Desert and Forest Reserve, created in 1870 UC by the first Amazian Emperor Hindonborg. Five hundred Sectals (395 miles) to the south is the famous Statue of Saturn, a colossal image of the ringed world carved from an extinct volcano by the financial wizard J. W. Wackon, to celebrate the Imperium's 100 birthday in 1967 UC. Nine hundred Sectals (710 miles) to the north are Lake Kygon and the Trifon Dam and Water Authority. This gigantic hydroelectric span provides irrigation to farms in the

Trifon Valley, which once was a vast sandbox of sterilized dirt. To the northeast, at four hundred Sectals (316 miles), between the cities of Markos, Batter, and Genson, is the Victonian Army Base Hindonborg. Alack grinned to himself, he knows this area from attending archeological digs and downloading lectures from the Norumian Antiquity Society of Markos. This entire area is filled with the buried infrastructure of that great mother civilization.

"We thought it would be good if you saw the scene yourself." Interrupted Bellyhon, "and I thought your brother would be joining us, Citizen Sandavon?"

"We're not on speaking terms," Curtly replied Alack.

"What a terrible tragedy befell Caroli Muadon," began Movallis, "she was at the site of our theme park at the Sasha Dunes when a construction crane collapsed, killing her instantly."

"The body was so smashed we thought a quick cremation was in order," Added Bellyhon, "restoring her by the coroner for an open casket funeral would be very costly. I made the call on this one, you do understand?"

"Of course, Sir, you did the right thing," Remarked Danice playing along.

'Good girl,' Thought Alack smiling activating his audio recorder.

"The theme park Motif Vastuum is building is centered around a fantastic discovery. Grewel Growlon, a famous explorer and brilliantine discovered a lost civilization predating the ancient Norumians. He's uncovered some remarkable things at the Sasha Dunes." The Security Chief sent a signal to his men to be ready when they landed at the locality.

'Starshit,' Thought Alack.  He remembered a documentary hosted by that imposter of an archeologist Growlon, who made fantastic claims, upsetting the professional antiquity establishment.  He was even given an award by a prestigious antiquity group at a dinner event.  Now he realized why one of the studio big shots was doing a double take, they wanted to add credibility to their fantasy.  'They are responsible for the deaths of several others because of this!'

A huge construction site crawled landward beneath them as the Zo car banked to a secluded place outside the fence.  Long sandy round duns are partly removed, revealing square foundations in a stacked array, several partial avenues are cleared, one long stretch is graced by flanking statues, and other parts have partially exposed structures.  All the heavy earthmoving equipment is parked neatly by trailers and supply depots.

"Impressive…" mumbled Alack activating the hidden video recording device in his belt, he knew only the engineers of Norume can build such things; there is no pre-Norumian race and no major Norumian city ever occupied this site.

As soon as the vehicle touched the ground a dozen security men with handheld pistols jumped surrounding them.  Danice and Alack are removed from the car at gun point.

"Prefect Bellyhon made a polite bow, "Sorry about this…" and he walked away to a gate in the fence.

"Prefect!" Gasped Danice.

"He's played his part, now I must play mine."  Movallis instructed two of his men to take Danice's purse and other items.  Alack is forced to remove his long bulbous coat, utility belt and other articles. Once Movallis is satisfied had his men push them towards a concrete half buried structure. "Since this is the last thing you'll see I will be like those villains in the old flicks, clearing my mind of my guilt." Standing by a massive cement and steel door, leaned against the exposed rebarb. "Your friend discovered the ancient civilization but found it's actuality an old movie set buried by a defunct film studio decade before Vastuum. Plus, the remains of those who didn't cooperate with their bosses…rather sloppy work by my predecessor, but that's been taken care of. Since Motif is pouring millions of credits into this enterprise, he wants no bitch to spoil it. So, she refused to make a deal and is removed."

"That's Caroli…" mutter Danice.

"But her death wasn't here, it was in the dormitory building?"

"Yes, very good Sandavon. We do all our dirty work in a controlled place."

"Dirty work…" Alack greeted his teeth, a deadly hostile frown. "Then why are we here? The past is full of shadows."

"How delightful! I can play to. Elementary, Sir." Movallis stroked the old cement carefully with his hand enjoying his chance to play act. He took on the verbal accent of a famous sleuth from the old televisior (tv) shows. "We found this old bunker going back to the Revolutionary days. A rather imposing den, which when seen from without, may joggle one's imagination. At first, we thought of removing this monstrosity, but behold, someone suggested we restore it. Who knows what sinister antics comes from within? Only the higher ones know. Some say it wouldn't fit in with the theme park, so we've decided to bury it…to shame, with you two in it!" Waving his finger in a leisurely manner his men pushed Alack and Danice into the gapping entrance. Before Alack could swing around and resist the massive door is rolled into place leaving them in darkness.

The only thing he heard is Danice crying.

Alack turned off his collar recorder and put his eyes to work.

His vision is a step above the normal humanoid optic nerve. He can see things in darkness no one else can. "Danice…don't move…stay where you are…this place is littered with all sorts of stuff." A musty stale odor of decay penetrated everything.

"Hold me…I'm scared!"

He made her sit on a large slab of cement once used as a stand for an anvil. "I don't want you to strain or sprain anything. When we leave here there's a Ranger Station five Sectals (3.9 miles) away."

"Leave! How? I can't see nothing!"

"A small stick can move the ass of an Herbivore..."

"That's all we need is one of your stupid sayings!"

"Be quiet Danice, I must think." He left her to explore. Going around carefully felt and saw heavy chains, hooks from the low ceiling, giant logs, large iron caldrons for smelting and piles of bricks that once were a forge. He came back to her removing his shoe. "I doubt this Sensor Dot will work in here..." Alack tried it but got no returning signal. "As I thought…" His mumble is reassuring.

"And who are you going to call! I'm sure Prefect Bellyhon will help you move that door?"

Realizing she was right, he placed it back in his heel.

Alack went to the door and studied it. His long clumsy piano fingers feeling the seams, the surface cement, and the sides, then decided to try.  Spiking his metabolic rate applied his terrible strength to push the door back on its rollers.  After several air-gulping tries could not budge it, so taking a few deep breaths through his shoulder at the reinforced stone surface, he only hurting himself in the effort.  Returning to Danice, he pulled his shirt off, asking her to rub his deltoid as he powered down his heart.

"Is it possible there is something you can't break?"

"They built them well during the age of chemical firearms."

"Better?  Say better!  How do we get out, Alack?"  She saw only darkness in front of her.  "How much air do we have?"

He saw her worried face, "if we don't talk a good hour or two…" a dark mask of fear and rising panic.  "They won't bury us until tomorrow."

"How do you know that?"

"When we flew over the construction site, no one was working, must be a paid holiday for the union workers, and I'm sure Movallis will not dirty his hands dragging mounds of dirt and stone."  Alack is up.  "They think they have us, no reason to hurry."

Danice felt his body's warmth, determination, and resourcefulness.  "Maybe there's something around here you can use to break down the door…"  She could not see the flash of an idea burst inside his head.  All she heard is chains moving, something heavy flying up and over, more chain rustic sounds, the lumbering of heavy wood, a deep clank of some iron surface and much grunting and groaning, then the noise of a heavy object hanging and more chains rattling.

"What are you doing now?  I can't see a thing!"

"I just put your suggestion into motion, Danice. I made a battering ram from the big tree logs, a smelting pot, and these chains. The whole thing is suspended from several hoist hooks in the ceiling. Hold your ears, this will hurt." A concussion of horrible drumming bangs began slowly. It built up to a body-wrenching blast shaking bone and sinew getting louder and louder. Then, a zigzagging crack, another ear numbing blast, and light shafts burst in with a blinding glare.

She felt a strong hand seize her and minutes later both stood outside in the refreshing air. "The Ranger Station is this way…" After using the sensor dot to notify them, he snatched her up in his powerful arms, "Come! They will meet us halfway." and dashed away at a fast run, putting as much distance from the bunker as he could.


"Did you know Sandavon was armed?" Mentioned Security Chief Movallis to Prefect Bellyhon in the chief engineer's construction trailer, "here, you're the police guy. Look at this."

Bellyhon took Alack's Higgon II pistol from the holster. "This…this is SSG issued." The Prefect's face drew a dumb look. "His belt…what's a salesman doing with our ordinance?"

"Don't ask me…check out the registry number with your office." Movallis called Marjer Herlon reporting on the situation, explaining in detail how both irritants have died. "I'll have our crews bury the bunker tomorrow morning first thing, talk to you later."

Bellyhon is flustered after talking to his office on his portafon (cell phone). "Do you know who we killed! Special Service Agent Alack Troyus! Sandavon is Troyus, not two brothers but one guy." Movallis's jaw dropped as he looked away in disbelief. "This guy is also the Park Land Ranger up at the Colossus Reserve…"

"Was the Land Ranger! Was the Special Service Agent, stay with me on this Cory. They ain't going no where's…"

"You idiot!" Bellyhon saw Alack's utility belt and a red light blinking on one of the components. "This is SSG issue and the recording mechanism is on! Everything we've said, our phone talk is evidence against us!"

"I'll take that." Alack entered the trailer with four-armed Land Rangers in their brown kaki uniforms. "And I'll take my ray gun. You can't have any of my stuff because the show is over!" Grabbing both items stood erect facing Movallis. "I arrest you in the name of the Emperor, for murder and attempted murder. For allowing citizen personal rights violated, for illegal sexual acts and for concealing a criminal. You have the right to an attorney according to the Zoferin laws of the State of Marhon. You have the right of appeal directly to the Imperial level. Anything you say or do will be held against you as evidence." Alack turned towards Bellyhon. "You Sir are under arrest for corruption and murder, defilement of your office and trust to the people of Amazia. The criminal acts so stated for Movallis are also charged against you. I place you under the jurisdiction of the Servispate Office of the Regent of Bylon and the Inspector Consul of Amazia." Alack held out his palm. "You're firearm and ID Card."

Not saying anything Bellyhon meekly handed over the badges of his office as the Rangers seized both men.

"The Prefect of Markos will be here to take them into custody. This is Alack Troyus, Special Services, ZZSPAR6 concluding my tribunal at the Sasha Dunes, this date and time."

"Ya'know Troyus," began Danice with a drink in her hand studying Alack in his red shorts lounging on the beach by his ranch house. "That was the first time I saw you incapacitated. You couldn't do nothing. No gun, no muscles, no utility belt, no sticks, only my suggestion got you moving. I think I've earned something."

Alack read various news bulletins on his Calcomp ignoring her remark. She must always get the upper hand and have the last word.

"If it wasn't for me, we would have died in that smelly, dark bunker."

He read what he wanted to read, catching up on his litigation news. "You owe me big time, Seminian." Her dainty lips puckered in a delightful, desiring advance. "Does this tell you anything?"

"You want to go fishing?"

"If I were Sara Klaron this drink would be all over your handsome face."

"If you were her, I wouldn't be here getting teased." Alack held up the Calcomp. "They arrested them all. Juballa Vastuum, Merril Edon…Meander will like that. Even Motif Vastuum is under indictment. Darius Movallis was shot and killed trying to escape from the Rangers, and Prefect Bellyhon has turned star witness after he made a plea deal with the Imperial prosecutor. Marjer Herlon, plus two other studio executives, are accused of murder and violating the sexual rights of those girls at the dormitory. As for that crazy building, it's going to be demolished when a new one is built."

Danice frowned, glaring down at him. "And what of poor Caroli? And all those others who were used as sex things to keep their jobs?"

"Their getting justice.  Seems they all got inspired and gathered together, even getting those who fled from there, and sign confessions for a class action suit against those indicted."  He glanced up at her in the lounge chair as she took the Calcomp and read the social columns. "Batter City has a new Prefect, they promoted from within, which is the right thing to do, and the Prefect of Markos City is handling this entire case.  When he's done, I doubt Vastuum will be making no more films for some time."

"You're wrong, Troyus..."  She swung the text screen around. "Motif's second son, Darilymor dropped his ass in his father's chair and announced a new film in the making.  'War Cry of the Patriot' about the raid Edvard Constonline led to seize a Shuton gunboat and attack the Unapiterians at Batter City.  Says here 'not only action-packed with historical accuracy but a shattering love triangle for the whole family to enjoy', want to see this one?  You can tell me what's real and what's fiction?"

"The closer you get to innocents the closer you achieve perfection."

"Thanks for spoiling this day with that!"


THE END

# THE DEMON STONE AFFAIR

By Ernest Velon


"This is the place, Alack m'boy…" T.A. Elanus pulled on his striped suit, making a few adjustments to the collar and sleeves. Alack Troyus eyed him from a glance, knowing the motions were hand signals to his hidden bodyguards that Marts had deployed. He told them to wait outside the quaint emporium. The avenue of shops and elegant storefronts brought buyers from all over Amazia to the 'Crescent Way', the most exotic and expensive merchandise district on the planet. This section of Newlon City is a Mecca for the rich, the famous, and the powerful, not to mention the criminal powerbroker in disguise. Some of these stores are mere fronts for illegal trades from the various black stellar markets that are web-like throughout the Imperium. Alack knew this little jaunt in the exclusive district is more than a sightseeing tour. He patiently waited for 'old thunder throat' to come around and give him an assignment. It has been three Amazian weeks (24 days) since he returned from the Vasquez Affair. One week to wind-down, another to rest, and by the third the itch returns for more action; more like a punishment for going at it on his own from the 'old man'. When the call came in, Alack, who was doing repair work on the roof of his home, he dropped everything and came.

"I thought we were to have lunch, Sir?" mumbled Alack as his belly alerted him. "Not shop around for jewelry." Gastric noises started their annoying rumble.

"There's an old proverb, 'it's good to never finish a project so you can always have something to do next.' This store has many items you should ingest than organic matter. Shut up and follow me, and leave your tectonic sounds outside."

Alack grumbled, expecting a big lunch, "I'm reliving all the food I ate last night. Is this going to take long?"

"Longer than what's on your mind." Both entered a dazzling marble and chrome styled store with cases of brilliant gems, cut sapphires, and settings of great beauty. A number of Guards seemed to watch the two men carefully as they navigated around more glass cabinets with tiaras, glittering crowns, bracelets of radiating colors, and many different rings. They ignored well-dressed Elanus but Alack in his dirty athletic walking shoes, black shorts, and torn gray sleeveless shirt eyed him suspiciously. T.A. nodded at a few store clerics as he led the way to the rear. The fact that none of the sales people of this high-class establishment accosted them told him this is staged, a setup in advance. Alack is aware of hidden surveillance cameras, of sections that can be closed off, and even of protective force field generators disguised as wall lamps. His keen eyes detected an elaborate security system that convinced him of the valuables surrounding him. "This is what I wanted you to see."

Two Guards came a little closer as T.A. eyed a glass dome enclosure on a black velvet pedestal. Under the curving shield, a gigantic reddish-orange crystal blazed as each round facet reflected the rooms light. It is as large as a small vase but totally unique in structure and multifaceted shape. Alack leaned in closer studying its interior and saw that light rays seemed to move inside as if it is alive. Carefully walking around, the scintillations seemed to take on different shapes, never repeating the same design, always something new, something enchanting and entrapping.

"It's…it's like a snowflake…it never creates the same image…"

"And that's why they call them Snowflake Stones, or what the Unapiterians labeled them, Nex Astorum, in our AV."

"Whatever…" Alack swallowed, a loud noise in the quietness of the place. "I know a little about stellar mineralogy, but this is totally different. What elements make it up?"

"Always the scientist? This is a stone of death, Alack. People have killed to possess it. The blood of many greedy humanoids and aliens stains its reputation. Throughout the ages since the Shutons, this gem has cost more lives than all those who died in the Toshivic Revolt. It's shrouded in legend and tales of horror from a planet that has been on our doorstep since the formation of the solar system." T.A. placed his hand on Alack's shoulder since the young man is bent over. The tensile strength of the skin under the unseemly shirt reassured him that this visit was not a waste of time. "Don't dwell upon its facets too long or it will engulf you." Alack quickly stood straight up, his tall 158 Illo height (over six feet) glaring down at T.A. The handsome face with the big brown eyes, flock of long auburn hair, high cheeks, and rounded chin, the chiseled features between a boy and a man, grinned at his Superior. "They say it has a magical spell; it has driven those with a lesser will mad."

"Then if it's so enchanting, we are fortunate there's only one."

"Well…not exactly…" T.A. started to walk away towards the

entrance.

"You mean there are more of these?" Alack followed. "How did this all start?"

"Devil Stones, a more accurate term.  Since you enjoy the historical, I give it to you.  Walk this way, Alack m'boy, and take your smell with you."  Alack followed his Boss out of the store.  "A recent dig on the charred remains of Altairs II discovered the bunker belonging to the Great Tyrant, Tielen Reiefereian, if I'm pronouncing his name right."

"That's Altairian…difficult language, the phonetics are all wrong."

"Your difficult, pay attention."  T.A. headed down the avenue in a slow stride.  "The year is 1981 UC, the place is Altairs II, or Amonia of the original Altairian home system, star Altairs.  The Regina Borfun places his friend on the throne of a Class C world.  He has a great reputation as a decent guy.  After a full year of brilliant political sanity, he wakes up one morning totally mad.  He starts a program of genocide, slave labor, and other social horrors.  The planet has many R & D facilities, and he uses his influence to force the scientists to make the worst bomb in the history of the Universe."

"You're talking about the TNFF Device?"

"Very good, Alack m'boy, but we call it the Cosmitic Bomb.  A nasty weapon that uses the two hydrogen atoms in water to create a plasma chain reaction that'll destroy the atmosphere and surface water of an entire world in seconds.  It'll leave a charred burnt-out cinder where once something wonderful was before."

"Didn't the G. A. and S. C. outlaw that weapon?"

"That came after the fact. Tielen threatens the homeworld with annihilation if Lintus Borfun doesn't meet his demands. Regina Borfun, a weakling, last of his line, tries to trick Tielen into a peaceful parley but blows the whole effort and loses an army. He seeks help from the international community, in a carefully surgical strike."

"Are we involved?"

"I think so, Zaterite still had his marbles eighty-some years ago. Anyway, Tielen discovers the international force landing on his planet, retreats to his bunker, and detonates the bomb. Altairs II is decimated, the army is gone, and the blast sent waves of shock throughout the solar system. Altairs IV and III suffer ecological damage, and even the main star begins to show signs of instability. Orbital standards begin to change by large percentages. Class A worlds slowly become D and E places."

"I read that the Altairians began considering abandoning their home system and moving to the Argius globular cluster (NGC-628) outside of the Fylight."

"I heard that too in 2029…but they have a different sense of time. Now we jump fifty-seven years to 2035 UC. A new autocrat called Gustia Hypon of Romar, capital of the Delorian Republic, the main star is Alterous, once a colony of the Altairians. Located at the tip of the northern arm of the Fylight galaxy (Milky Way), is independent of the claws of the Regina. A great man and sensible ruler of a fragment of the old Unapiterian Empire, and here again, he wake's up one morning raving mad. A simple spy incident with his neighbors the Altairians sends both nations into war. The Alto-Delorian War of 2035 saw the unleashing of terrible weapons. Both sides used the Cosmitic bomb wrecking three Class A worlds in less than an Agel."

"And you blame this on the Devil Stones?"

"The Altairian Regina went insane, Tielen went mad, and Hypon ended up hanging himself. These stones were found in a necklace, on a medallion, and in the bunker of Tielen. We even think, after careful research, that the stone we just saw belonged to one of Zaterite's mistresses. His paranoia didn't become serious until 2009, when she was seen by his side."

"So, there are many more?"

Unfortunately, they have appeared on every major planet in the Imperium, and beyond." Alack almost ploughed into T.A. as he stopped. "The throne of Altairs has one, when we conquered Oreyomia (NGC-600) in the 2040's the crown of the Shintos had a big setting. All the Celestial King-Emperors of Unapiteria, from Barter's onward, topped their scepters with this gem. Even the Veonian Starkons had one in their diadems. Every monarch or autocrat we have records on these stones is there. "Even the Suberalivus Sword, our magical sword from the last Victin of Norume, had a Devil Stone placed on the hilt as a symbol of divine power."

"I've read, Sir, in Zaterite's last years he wore the Sword all the time. You're saying that between his mistress and the State Sword he suffered from madness late in life?"

"Or driven to it." T.A. stopped and gave eye contact. "Some unknown agency, right after the Unapiterian conquest, began spreading them to habitable worlds as the Empire expanded. When we came along, this unknown agency continued behind Zaterite's expansion on into our time."

"Sir, you've called me a little weird, or a religious romantic, but I'm sure there's a medical and scientific explanation to all this. The past is full of shadows."

"Okay, Alack, I'll play in your shadowy park. In the Kudor Thor Affair, what was the evil wizard Morasha wearing when she seduced you?" Alack's big brown eyes wandered into them selves trying to recall. "If that doesn't jog your memory in the Praxis Affair what was the Lizyonites wearing around their greedy necks?" Alack's eyes went wide in revelation. "Behold, a light shines within! There's more to life than the noise from your gut. Now that we have some basis for an understanding, I'll continue. As far as I know these Devil Stones are still being sold and distributed."

"But by who, Sir?"

"That's what you're going to find out." T.A. pushed Alack's muscular bulk into the restaurant. "See, smell that! I've never let you down, Alack m'boy. All's well that eats well."

Returning home with the purple pouch of data crystals Alack finished his roof work, showered and changed into his kimono for relaxation. He poured himself a glass of DeMassie wine. Going to his Spartan desk and work area on the raised portion of his living room, tackled the new assignment.

T.A.'s data was very historical but lacked certain details he sought. It seemed as the Unapiterians conquered the Fylight galaxy (Milky Way) and made interstellar travel easy for merchants, so did the secret agency spread these crystals about. As Elanus mentioned, the expansion of Amazia under Zaterite and Dwitinton added to the popularity of acquiring them for royalty and the mega rich. Whoever these agents are have done an exceptional job of selling them to the right people.  Going to the Library Net and other sources of cosmic information, Alack sought a clue to who these people might be.  All records are the same, no mention of a group of gem merchants or even a source from a mine.

Shifting gears, Alack went into the scientific data circles of geology and mineralogy to find more hard facts on these Demon Stones.  To his surprise, they are not considered a mineral crystal.  Gems and crystals are made from slow-cooling magma from volcanic fissures.  Some stones come from Thermopile reaction with microbes and minerals.  Then there are Magnatomics, an ion particle breakdown of rare elements to produce opticals.  The more exotic crystal formations from ammonia and nitrogen inter-reacting with the Titanium Nitride chains at subzero temperatures came very close to the unique facets of the Devil Stones.  Industrial made variants looked okay but every shape had an Ingram of identification stating specifics and manufacturer.  Alack even looked at Bio-Mechanics, the science of fertilizers that grow pure chemical crystal compounds.  In the end, different environments and their elements grow a vast variety of fabulous stones from countless planets, but they all cannot compare to these.  These Nex Astorum stones grow in a different manner entirely.  Comparisons are made to the warm water pearl, the salt water blue diamond, the sapphire of yellow sulfur springs and dozen more.  One small creature, a variety of the same species, excretes their byproducts around a tiny grain of sand and over the course of many years and layering, makes a valuable stone.  The mother creature dies leaving behind the lifelong handy work of their septic existence.

"These things are not grown by a life form and not created in a slow cooling magma furnace..." mumbled Alack falling back into his Captain's chair. "They have round convex and concave facets, not flat or triangular, almost non-Euclidian." He sipped the long stem wine glass slowly. "No industrial lab can make these...the natural laws don't apply here." His mind raced down corridors, opening and closing doors, finding another hallway leading off to more portals. Eventually, it all led in the same direction, a great big question mark. "I need to go back to that store and question the owner...and use my mind and Calcomp to analyze the stone...maybe..."

Next day, dressed in his field clothes, black pants, black shoes, and white short sleeved polo shirt with his rank on the collar, Calcomp strung over his broad shoulder, Alack entered the jeweler's store on Crescent Way. This time, a store Salesman intercepted him as his toes touched the inner carpet. Alack flashed his credentials and asked to see the main gem of their collection.

"Oh yes, I remember you, anything for Lord Elanus. Follow me."

'Good boy...' thought Alack as he allowed his small guide in the long Lizyonite frock coat to lead on. 'T.A. has them trained well.'

Again, they stopped at the pedestal with the curving glass dome and shell. There, resting in vast orange splendor and eye-catching silver scintillations, is the Devil Stone.

"Dyabilus Nex Astorum, the Devil's Snow Star..." Alack unstrung his Calcomp and made a few adjustments, "and what by Arathon are you doing, Sir?"

"I want to scan this…"

"That won't work, we've tried."

Not taking no for an answer, Alack activated his pencil directional wand and frowned over the readings. Making a further adjustment switched quanta particles to a deeper neutrino one. Again, the image blurred and error messages filled the rectangular screen. Making a loud snort, Alack played with lower simple frequency waves and fields but achieved the same results. In a final effort, he did a very photonic laser sweep but had his concentrated beam reflected off. Not since the Munshine and Fennox Affairs has his device been confounded. Making a loud 'harrumph' sent his mind out only to have it kicked back by some unusual psychic whip. A brief headache told him this was a mistake.

"I told you so!" stated the Salesman seeing Alack's handsome face creased in pain.

"Let me see your Lapidarist?"

"Oh my, you are persistent. Walk this way, Sir."

In a small room with a long, curving desk, various devices for cutting and polishing, and shelves of finished and half completed jobs, sat a small Amazian with a wrinkled face. "I'm the owner, Frayshon, what do you want?" Alack flashed his credentials and told him of his efforts. "You're not the only one who tried. Those in our craft like to know what we're getting but that demon stone won't reveal its composition!"

"So, there's no real analysis, your saying, Sir?"

"Well…" he closed the door, locking it. "I did a bad thing Colonel Troyus, when I acquired the stone, I took a part of the bottom off after my scans went the way of yours. I pulverized it and did a spectronic Tomography, very unorthodox and unheard of, but it worked, and I got what I wanted." He went to a safe concealed in a coffee cabinet. "Since your Boss has bought many prized things from me and referred the Victonian Eagles to my simple little shop, I owe him big time." He gave Alack a data crystal on the Devil Stone. "I'm assuming very few have this, and I want it back when you're done."

Alack removed his Calcomp, inserted the data piece, and downloaded all chemical information. Stretching a broad grin, gave it back.

"He said you were unique…"

As he secured it in the safe Alack studied the charts and percentages. "This is organic, not inorganic. These chains of compounds…I've never seen, and I know a little of the sciences. Time and consciousness are relative."

"A master blend of rare earths, long chains of the cosmic, and valences that shouldn't be…forged in the heart of an exploding star, a true stone of the Devil himself. Would you like to know how I got it?"

"Yes! Say it or delay it, if you please, Sir!"

"Would you believe me if I told you it fell from the sky?" Alack frowned, "I thought so. Ten years ago, I was at a religious retreat to cure some ailments that local doctors said my insurance didn't cover. I was in this mineral bath when something splashed beside me. It was that stone. While I lay in the waters a minor trembler shook the building and dislodged something from above. Into my lap it fell, a gift of their God, long since buried to be revealed again."

"We're you on Amazia or off-world, Sir?"

"Amtor, the Temple of the White Waters, health spa and casino, you'll love it."

The first recorded evidence of humanoid life began on Amtor (Venus) some four thousand seven hundred and sixty-two years before the creation of the Universal Calendar by the Norumians on Amazia. A Class A and B world on the Crompton Scale, Amtor has a very unique environment as compared to other planets harboring life. She glides in an elliptical orbit in and out of the Habitation Zone around Mytia. A hot box with an average rotation of forty-eight hours, equatorial temperatures vary from over a hundred degrees to ninety in the shade. All inhabitances are in the northern and polar hemispheres, as the tropical oceans feed the weather system with continuous rain.

Amtor's core is alive but declining. Her internal fires are not what they were but add to the surface temperatures and create the magnetosphere, which protects the planet from solar activity. The scattering of large islands and tectonic activity is mostly null and underwater. With a dense atmosphere, twice the norm for humanoids, Amtor reflects more light and heat than any other planet in the solar system. With thirty some land mass islands making up the surface, a vast ocean of warm water engulfs eighty percent of the planet. Great strains of giant algae and sea lichens, mutated from eons of evolution, swept over the flat islands and hugged the coastal shores. They trapped the heat, cooling off sections of the northern and polar zones. Providing a hearty source of food for those who adapted and survived, a leftover race of humanoids, planted eons ago by the Great Krill, became maritime nomads.

The first people who developed a civilization were the Kazels. The first recorded person, the 'Speaker' discovered a rectangular lake on the island of Usar. At the bottom of this shallow manmade lake are stone squares with writing. By some psychic means, so the legends state, he translated the stones and wrote the book of Havihej, the Amtorian guide to a happy life. Over centuries of further study, those who settled by the lake became 'teachers' and 'priests' and they created a monastery dedicated to the God of the White Water. With a rudimentary awakening, the Kazels built the first nation on Amtor. With new knowledge, they expanded over the hot waters in reed ships and founded many colonies.

One of these settlements, the Monberns (wanderers) returned to Usar as conquerors and seized control of the nation. They built the first major city called Senacia around one thousand two hundred years before the Calendar. They expanded the temple complex using it to control the scattered island settlements. This gave rise to a powerful hierocracy of nobles and lords who eventually abused their power. They ruled as tyrants until a third tribe, the Ancars rose in revolt and overturned the ruling cast. The Ancars seized the temple complex and organized the scattered colonies on the island into a more unified nation. In 450 U.C. they founded the capital Ancar as the central authority of their government.

The new Ancar civilization (also known as the Szankkasia) flourished for over a thousand years, learning from and adapting to the harsh planetary environment. In 1510 U.C. the Unapiterians invaded and established planetary rule under the Shutons. Finding Amtor a good place to vacation and enjoy the tropical conditions, made it a pleasure spot for their elite. They discovered the White Water Lake, the monastery, and the old priestly order. Capitalizing upon this, the Unapiterians expanded the new knowledge found within the writing under the waters. Scientists made astounding discoveries, enhancing technology and advancing further to the stars.

In the 1830's, the revolts on Amazia, Barsoom (Mars) and Altairs swept away the Shutons, and the Unapiterian Empire was fragmented. But the new Amtorian Eparch retained their Shuton governors more as a ceremonial attachment to the regime of the Ancars. In 1979, Shuton Kar-Mandaria rallied the Army of Amtor in a brief conflict with the Bitery Nation, carving out a sliver of spatial solar systems. Soon after, Amtor established her full independence as a recognized planet by joining the Space Council with many others. But the last holdout of the Shutons did not leave Amtor until 2016 U.C., they had become political figureheads along with the Palasatro Guards. Once their influence over the Ancars was gone, the planet became a major vacation resort. Today, Amtor exports a host of organic drugs and herbs farmed from the gigantic algae choking her coastal waters. Add to that a vast variety of aquatic foods and specialty items the wealthy seek.

It is here that Alack Troyus found himself in his quest to learn the secrets of the Devil Stones.

Ancar City is mostly underground on the main island of Usar. The coolness of the subterranean caverns makes life pleasant. Volcanic vents throughout the world suck in the hot air and force it out as a chill, cooling down the overheated atmosphere. Without this natural process, Amtor's surface temperature would be around five hundred degrees. Because of latent tectonic activity, this unique cooling system acts as a below ground weather system, constantly cycling the atmosphere. Add to the oxygen generating algae, Amtor has supported a controlled population of one billion.

Alack, carrying his single valise, made his way amongst the ninety-six Illo (4 feet) Amtorians. Recalling the Karactikas Affair and his encounter with the Amtorian Fraskia from Salak City, who broke into his room in Cape May on Terra, he realized how small these people are. Humanoid, but skinny, with small heads, big bodies and limbs to match, their faces are kind of flat, with recessed eyes, a thin mouth, ears that curl inwards and a firm bushel of dark black hair. They all had the same hair! Their faces are somewhat different, each individual unique, but the hair, the same weird bell-shaped style. Even the children have that round egg flock; the face almost hidden amongst the straight bangs.

The Amtorian clothes are as few as possible because of the high humidity and heat. Alack once again gravitated toward the physical study of those who developed a fine physique and those who were gross and fat. Sandals with shorts, a belt with hanging items, reminded Alack of the equatorial tribes of Seminia. A strange, rough odor of perfume mixed with unwashed body smells twitched his sensitive nose, reminding him of the Amtor Trap Plants Danice has. He also recalled the monstrosities created by a group of ill-advised university students in the Mooselose Affair, who created a gigantic carnivorous plant that threatened the Amazian biosphere. Returning to the Amtor squawking tongues made a weird bleating sound as he carefully moved amongst them. Use to aliens and strangers, the Amtorians ignored the tall Seminian hurrying around his stout legs.

Finding the Hotel of Amtor, Alack checked in.

Before going to the surface, he wanted to spend a day acclimating himself to this new environment. Amtor has higher atmospheric pressure, just over two Atmospheres for Class A-C planets within and on the edge of the Habitation Zone (about 27 lbs per sq inch). His studies told him to allow over thirty hours to get used to the density. But the advice is for normal humanoids, not the tougher Seminian hide. His home world has one and a half Atmospheres, which helped Alack adapt quickly. Since Amtor is not within the Imperium, Alack had to get a number of inoculations that made his belly do flip-flops. Health and hygiene standards are different for each planet beyond the borders of Amazia.

'These are the people of Havihej…I've never read their holy book, but we have a higher standard of living than this…' thought Alack as he checked out the small hotel room. Designed for foreigners and aliens of bigger stature, it is a random mess of adaptable furniture. The toilet is both a shower and bathtub, with a walk-in door and curtain affair. But the bed is expandable and hard, just the way he likes it. After settling in, Alack adjusted his Calcomp to the different power settings and downloaded the applications to access the planetary ServNet. Amtor used an older quadratic code for processing, not the progressive Decca systems that exist on Amazia. 'Thank Arathon for backup software…'

Alack had done his research before leaving Amazia but always double-checked again for accuracy. He found the Amazian database on Amtor incomplete. Entire sections are poorly revealed, with cities and islands not where they are meant to be. But he checked out the travelogue sites for merchants and acquired a detailed picture.

'Interesting…maybe I'm not supposed to go to certain places here…' The Temple of the White Waters is two places not one. An older restored complex is located north on the main island of Usar, the other, a health spa and casino entertainment theme park is on the second island of Simparto, near Cimparto City.

Something told Alack to go-to the older place, up north.

He knew the water tablets and the square lake were the real places he must seek. Also, the Venusian writing under the water is very similar to the ancient script of the Norumians of Amazia. That is why their ancient language is called AV, Ancient Venusian. 'According to archaeological theories, the Krill civilization left them there as a vault of information. These things appear all over the General Group of galaxies (Local Group). This I must see.' Alack checked on Silorian (land) transport to Digar, a city near the square lake. A monorail leaves Ancar every day on a twenty-hour trip at high speed. Making arrangements for the next day, Alack sought out the nearest restaurant.

A sad faced Waiter in a neck collar, waist gown, and sandals guided Alack to a lay-down bed that can be folded into several positions for eating. After adjusting for a chair, the arm swung over as a table. He ordered the local seafood dishes, several of them because the portions are terribly small. Then a host of expensive pastries since grain products are imported. He tried the 'sea bread', a special algae seaweed that is processed into a fine muffin and baked. Alack inhaled a dozen before he is satisfied. The sour face of the Waiter almost enclosed in a teardrop of black hair actually smiled up.

Alack returned a goofy grin with a pleasant expression.

The next Amtorian day (two Amazian days) Alack boarded a

monorail for a trip to Digar, an interior city of the Usar Island. A special coach for taller aliens and visitors had been added, with reclining seats, snack trays, and a strange series of vending machines at both ends with facilities. The other cars attached are for the Amtorians themselves. Two levels within, with horizontal seats and feeding tubes and entertainment devices in the ceilings. Other cars have one level with the same type of seats but more room for personal items like luggage, children, and even domesticated animals. Alack discovered a favorite snack food is a live, half mud rodent half fish creature called a 'flapper'oth' that lives on both lands and in the sea. They are eaten live and are very messy, even when the parents sharing pieces with their children.

Alack frond the travel and tourist videofons by Amtorians are incorrect.

These showed lush vacation and tropical settings with gleaming hotels and exciting water sports. What he saw was stark rocky blackish gray, broken hills, no mountains. Occasional valleys with some type of fauna resembling a large fungus mushroom plant and the crawling Amtorian spice tree. Since tectonic activity is mostly underwater, the constant rains and mists washed away all gravel and topsoil, leaving dull, ugly basement rock exposed. In more wealthy areas, ocean filler, dredged from the sea's bottom, filled depressions, creating farms and fruit gardens. But this is something only the rich and powerful in Amtorian society can afford.

The lack of mountain ranges made the weather and climate a constant haze of whiteness throughout the world. As the equatorial belt received the bulk of constant monsoon rains, the northern and southern temperate polar regions received a mist. Like a great cloud covering them, it crawled over the islands in the early morning and by noontime had ascended upwards to about seven thousand Sectals (almost six miles). Hanging like a great obscuring sheet of mist Amtor's skies are a constant whiteness shrouded in obscurity. Like on other Class A, B or C worlds, there's no blue or green, or reddish scattering of light. Here, all is a pastel whiteness with reduced color renditions. Another reason why the Amtorians are color blind or so diluted they no longer see like other humanoids.

Alack noticed this right away. A drabness in fashions, buildings, and signs seemed to be accepted by all inhabitants. Many societies paint their buildings, statues, and monuments in vivid colors, here, only a grayish stone luster remains.

The air conditioner system made the coach to cold. When the monorail arrived at Digal Alack felt relief as a blast of hot, humid air struck his skin. Dressed in his white walking rubbery shoes, white athletic socks, black shorts, utility belt and white polo short sleeved shirt, he brought his valise and Calcomp. Getting stares and squints the Seminian ignored the Amtorians studying him. Even the other visitors and aliens aboard the coach are not as big as he is. But, when they saw his flock of long well-groomed hair, a flash of white teeth, considered a sign of approval, stretched their sour little faces.

'Long well styled hair is an asset here…' thought Alack as he looked for a restaurant, 'these people aren't so bad after all. A positive thought is a positive way.'

The funny little village of Digal is above ground. For some reason atmospheric pressure is a little less in the northern and southern regions below the poles. Cities along the equatorial islands are all subterranean affairs going down to cooler caverns and vast empty fissures. It is said there are entire below ground seas and lakes that channel the hot surface drafts to a colder gust. Further pressure pushes these thermal cycle systems to the atmosphere making things slightly cooler. But Digal and other villages are surface affairs.

Fairy like, with conical pavilions with no windows, they curved and squatted like a mess of fallen toys. The simple roads and paths led in all directions. If it was not for the tourist map Alack purchased, he would never find an eatery suitable for his kind. The ashen block and round inn are big and roomy, with an upstairs for guests. Checking in at the front desk, which serves as a bar and food counter Alack ordered enough to feed two large families. A strange hodgepodge of giant snails, fungi cooked in a bread mix, plus many small fruits and vegetables, finally filled him. The menu had other items from different worlds that are popular with the tourists but Alack wanted to test the gastric waters of a different culture.

The sour faced Waiter actually broke a grin when he was paid.

Going to his room, adjusted the furniture and moved things around. To his dismay, there is no ServNet broadcast receivers in this isolated area. His Calcomp was useless for long distance or off world communications. Only in the major cities there are comm. links on the buildings and geosynchronous satellites in orbit. 'Oh well…' thought Alack, 'guess I've got to rough this alone. When in Norume do as they do.'

After a nap, Alack gathered what he needed and left for the monastery about a Sectal from the village. 'No wonder why they have very little art here,' thought Alack as a blast of heavy humidity hit him like a wall. 'Who can be inspired with such a dreary sky and landscape?'

The paved road suddenly ended outside the town's periphery and became slabs of that ashen bedrock. Taking a small sample Alack sat down on a boulder, accessed the geological data base of his Calcomp and did a quick analysis. 'Wow…this stuff is awfully hard.' He studied the squashed crystalline strata, a vast compression of igneous layers over millions of years. 'This has gone through tremendous pressure…when the planet was more active tectonically.' Alack brought up a comparison program of other similar minerals. 'This stuff is almost like Amazian Basement Rock, squashed and compressed under great tectonic heat and pressure. If all this is the same worldwide it is the oldest and hardest rocks on Amtor.' Alack tossed the piece aside.

"Hey, Asshole…look before a toss!"

Alack shot to his big feet.

"You think I ain't here because we be so small?" A chubby Amtorian wobbled up to him. "You big fuckers think you own the Universe, well, eat this!" He jabbed his fingers in his mouth in the standard Amtorian insult.

"Sorry, I didn't see…" Alack adjusted his ear translator.

"Excuses and more excuses. Say there, you're not the normal ones who come here to look? Your different, you got hair!"

Alack re-strung his Calcomp over those broad shoulders. "I'm Seminian, not Amazian…"

"Never heard of them peoples but you're welcome."

"Long hair amongst my race is a status symbol of our manhood." Alack gave him his goofy smile with the ends of his lips pushed up.

"Also, a warrior's pride."

"A fighter?  Good, where do you go?  I'm walking to the White Waters to make a prayer and donation."

"Then we can go together as one.  I too am going to the Lake of the Letters."

"You armed?"  They started on their trek.

"No…" lied Alack, "but I can handle myself…"

"Good."

"Are there two-legged dangers along this way?"

"Only the Alphases.  They in their hotness for a mate, stay out of the jungle."

Alack paused, he knew that name, and the carnivorous plant from the Mooselose Affair crystallized in his mind.  "Are you talking about the Amtor Trap?"

"They are in season and hungry, quick and sweet they are, but beware, some call them Crawling Rafflesia, stay on the road if seen."

"Will they attack people?"

"It depends on what they want.  I'm Dapo Maharatta Usaranzeritti, but Dapo calls me."

"Alack Troyus from Amazia…"

"I heard from Seminia, what happened, you're mind you changed?"

"No…I mean, Seminia is my native home and the racial world, Amazia is where I live and work."

"Still messed up, you weird!  What do you do?"

"I work for an import export company…"

"Still messed up not right. Either you receive or send, your mind, make it up."

Alack exhaled and changed the subject. "What's your profession, Dapo?"

"I'm the local worrywart, the town Prako (Crier), I tell them what's they like to hear in the morning as the mist settles in and in the evening when it hangs high above."

"In my home village on Seminia we have the same. The fellow is the local policeman under the Vilamaster. He is also…"

"Do they pay well? Two jobs, two bags of money?"

"No, one salary covers all…"

"I never go there, it's too cheap and messed up." They came to a crevice the road was cut through. By the marks in the stone wall, many tools with many hands did the digging. "They wait for us here. A fight to occur."

No sooner said when four almost naked Amtorians jumped down, blocking the lessening road. They stood in martial arts pose with hands and feet crouched. Three whipped out a weapon similar to a Seminian Kor-Hung, two metal laced sticks connected by a chain. They swung it between their waists, underarms, and above the heads, making strange clicking sounds.

Alack started to laugh.

"You stupid messed up! They mean to hurt."

"Sorry about that…but I've seen this before…on another planet…" more laughter. His translator had problems interpreting the lower Amtorian dialects. Only the main tongue is discerned, not the lower sub tongues. Amtor is not a major world where many languages are spoken and required to know when doing business. "Sounds like they are forceful…but the best of men fears nothing." Alack stepped forward, puffed up his chest, sent his mind out to receive impressions, and got whacked in the face. The Kor-Hung cut a welt of skin from his high cheek, just missing the jugular.

Animated, Alack went down in a crouch, lashed out with his fist and tossed the little Fellow against the nearest rock. Another hit him in the deltoid with the weapon. Alack spun on the ball of his boot, kicked up, and disarmed the other guy. He caught the Kor-Hung in flight. A strong yank and it left the little Guy's hand. Gyrating quickly swung the weapon wide, striking two sour-faced Amtorians under their flat noses. Within minutes, they backed off, grabbed the fallen, and ran away.

Alack stood rubbing his cheek as the skin healed quickly. "I'll keep this…" he examined the Kor-Hung and its weird writing along the shafts between the laced studs. "We may need it again." To his dismay, Dapo ran off with the robbers. "That little guy was part of this! Fruit and shit go together."

Feeling annoyed, he pressed onwards to the monastery and lake with determination.

Arriving in a small, vegetated valley, he saw the conical roofs and rounded pavilions nestled amongst the prickly spice tree forest, no taller than himself. Further down is a rectangular man-made pond stretching off by about half a Sectal. The greenish waters are calm, and below them, golden squares glistened. "So…this is where Ancient Venusian comes from, the written tongue of the great Krill, so some scholars believe…" A burst of weakness seized him. Gurgling up from his belly, Alack realized he was starving. 'Must be this drab environment…ugh…the shakes are starting…' But his disciplined thoughts gave him a temporarily advantage.

"Hey, you!  Want anything to eat?"  An Amtorian peddler pushed his cart forward.  Dressed in only a g-string he opened his compartments to display his wares, saying, "just got a fresh sponge, Kalla, and the sauce from the brine."

Feeling utter relief, Alack ordered large portions of everything. "Are you from the Temple of the White Waters?"  He barely got the words out between swallows.

"I'm the Anonmin, my job is to feed the travelers…"  Alack made a pig of himself, his eyes are always bigger than his belly.  "How can you eat so much and not get fat?"

"I burn it off very fast.  Got anything to drink?"

Try a homemade brew of leaf tea."  Alack emptied the entire decanter.  "You eat to much, got to go back and get more…"  Feeling slight remorse over his appetite, he forced payment upon the Fellow.  Claiming it-was a big tip, he wobbled off, pushing his empty cart back to the sanctuary.

"I live to eat…" mumbled Alack feeling the stuff digest away in his hyperactive stomach.  "After that…now I know I can digest anything!"  Feeling renewed, he went back to the finely cut squares about twenty-four Illos (1 foot) beneath the waters.  He noticed how clean and algae free they are.  Out on the expansive lake, he heard a splashing sound.  There, a raft with Amtorians holding big sponges dove and ascended, removing debris and gently cleaning the slabs.  They are totally naked, with their hair bunched up in a pinhead look.  "They must be from the Temple, but their actions are hesitant…they don't look normal.  Doing their penance to the God of the Waters?"

Alack took out his Calcomp and began some scans of the tablets near the shore. The software, designed by the late Octor, removed the diffraction caused by the density of water and presented a clear, undistorted image. 'Definitely the written script of the Norumians …the letters are bold and perfect…Peptillian discovered the same writing on Amazia and other worlds…' A new thought entered his excited mind, 'this proves a lake of this type, which the Krill called a 'vault', was left on Amazia also. What we thought was an underground facility is a surface lake. One of the ancient tribes of Norume copied this but the lake sight is long gone, the original squares scattered, and the style was used for legal documents.' Alack stood, beginning to pace as he went deeper into his hobby. 'This confirms everything! Even the edicts of the Victins were always perfectly square, plain, and bold. The early laws the founding fathers of Norume placed in the market square for the public to see and read are also the same fonts and styles…'

His pacing is now almost a run.

'But the evolution of the spoken script must be way off…' Alack went back to his Calcomp studying the square entablatures. 'The Amazian alphabet has twenty-seven letters and three symbols for punctuation marks, and is phonetic. The Norumians had the same as we, borrowed from other tongues with additions over the centuries and further defined by the Unapiterians. But, if this is the original written script of the Great Krill, they have the right letters, but they are all jumbled up!' Alack sat down on a rock, channeling more energy into his thinking. 'What little we know is that they had six hundred letters but only used over twenty, and ten other symbols, four of which are for punctuation, but the other six are some kinds of action preceded by other letters of thoughts.  But the Great Krill abolished a written language just before their annihilation.  If the theory of the genetic plague is correct, the Krill knew they are dying and made these water vaults to assist the people they planted on certain vacation worlds, like Amazia.  Half a million years is a long time, even the master had compassion for the slave.  Damn…if only Meander Astrikon was here, he'd flip out!'

Alack is now up stringing his Calcomp over a broad shoulder. 'No one knows what original Krill language sounded like…'  Turning away from the lake, he saw the Temple complex and headed quickly up the trail.  A tiny voice entered his mind, reminding him of the original mission and the Demon Stone.  'Maybe there's a connection?'  He fired back as his long well-groomed hair bounced with every footstep.

The trail became broken flagstones, worn and polished by countless bare feet.  As he neared the main entrance, a small, ugly rodent with a long tail and horrible whiskery face scurried before his boots. "Ah!  Annala Rodnostos, the Venusian Rat, I know of you!" He recalled the longest running challenge of his career, the Day-Zano Affair.

A vestibule loomed under a great canopy of fern bushes and spider algae.  It is vaulted, with plenty of head room for a 158 Illo (over six feet) tall Seminian.  On the curving walls are polished stone panels, hundreds of them on both sides, ending just before the apex of the ceiling.  Each panel is in Ancient Venusian.  When Alack compared the ones from the shore line of the lake to these, he found they were identical.

'Reproduced here for the traveler or the priests to study…'  He quickly began a full digital sweep, moving a few Illos forward, getting both sides, with his Calcomp.  When done, he found a secluded courtyard to look at his images. Alack recalled the evolution of writing from his linguistic studies in archaeology. 'Writing began by bookkeepers and merchants on most humanoid worlds. A simple way of counting and symbols of items bought and sold, or bartered. As trade became more specialized and civilizations advanced, other symbols were added to show different transactions. This led to pictographs and then hieroglyphics becoming complex as symbols began to be combined to form a thought or idea. Since there were no dictionaries to formalize a standard, each generation changed the symbols slowly as time moved on. As society became more complex symbols changed to letters, and from this, literature and legal documents evolved. A great sophistication of a civilization's ability to be creative is the development of an alphabet.' Alack had a feeling as the jumbled letters defied his attempts of translating. 'I need a better processor than this…my Calcomp can do it but it'll take hours.'

A sudden whiff of cooking peaked his nose. Alack stood, patting his belly. 'This food goes right through me…' He saw a cloud going up beyond a wall. 'Where's there's smoke there's dinner!' and began to seek a way around the source.

Admits a great bellowing of greasy, oily clouds and much squealing noise, Amtorians called Villicus, leaders of local lands, danced around the altar. A gigantic whale like animal, with fins resembling paws and a skin between that of a mammal and aquatic creature, is carved by the Arkgalus, assistant high priest. Small flat dishes are handed out as a long line of Amtorians gathered for a feast. Seeing a Buffet table further down is filled with a vast variety of exotic foods, Alack quickly leaped to the end of the line.

They served him.  Cute bell haircuts, ruddy smiling faces, beady recessed eyes, all seemed happy to please the tall Stranger with a fine smile and long well-groomed hair.

With almost a dozen plates, Alack found a small, secluded open cubical and sat down to eat.  He inhaled everything quickly going back for seconds and thirds.  The only dish he refused was a cooked Venusian Rat.  When full, stretched out on the stones, and digested.  He really piled it on.  Forcing his never satisfied belly to new shapes, a bloated mass now gnawing and straining at the skin of his abdomen muscles; Alack gently gave a sigh of relief.  Since arriving on Amtor whatever he ate never quelled the fires down below.  There are no grains or rice products, fruit and vegetables are small and seedy, meats and poultry are fishy type of animal, and the vast variety of algae-based foods do nothing for his hyper-active metabolic system.  'Damn… can't wait to get out of here and return home for a sizzling steak!  I am what I eat…'

Two Mistugogi Priests with spiked clubs glared at him.

Alack turned his handsome face, bringing it to eye level, and gave them his best goofy grin.

"Why do you partake of the ceremony?  The sacrificial food is only for those who make a long hazardous journey."

"You have no worth; we want all back!" chirped the other almost growling.

Making a grin with the ends of his lips up, Alack moved like lightning and stood towering over them.  They fell back, their pudgy almost naked bodies banging into one another, the clubs going down.  "But I to have made a great and dangerous journey from Amazia…uh…you have heard of that place?"

Others quickly joined them.  They put their heads together and began a bobbing routine of prayer and thought.  A few minutes after this, they separated, smiling and showing mucus membranes where teeth once were.  "We be very sorry and ask forgiveness."  They said as one.

"Very few from off worlds come here."

"They go to vacation and warm waters down south."

"They are not interested in heritage."

"Only in pleasures of flesh…"

"But I want to know your heritage, can you guide me?" grinned Alack.

"I shall get Hishtar lead you through the Stones of Eternity, come."

Alack followed, and relieved that this ended in a peaceful manner.

At first, the Seminian thought they were playing a trick on him, as did the fellow on the road, but was introduced to the Hishtar, the High Priest of the Temple.  He led him down the long-curved tunnel to the entrance of the complex.  But the Fellow abruptly halted and began pointing his metal staff at the first stone panels.  "Begins it here, a million lifetimes ago, the Great Villars, which others call Krill, carved in mystic stone these symbols.  They tell wonders of the world, how to hunt, how to cook, how to build, and how to live.  For lifetimes untold we have been sacred guardians of Lake and the White Waters.  The ravages of Kazels, the plunderings of Monberns, Shutons and final settlements of Ancars have made us stronger and more persistent in our ways.  Even under the Nefastas (bad spirits) of Shutons we survived."

"The Unapiterians were here also?"

"They were worst. They came and took sacred Jars of the very early Villar Ancients. They no idea what they unleashed upon themselves…"

Alack frowned down at him. "What Jars of the ancients?"

"It even older than planet Amtor. The Great Villars changed the order of heavens to make the world as it is. We have tried to understand, but even amongst our kind these stones are mere translations of those under waters. We have copied all perfectly, but some, we know not what we do. There are mysteries our minds can as of yet, not fully know. Things under the mist are hidden and gray of form."

Alack's mind burst into high gear.

He knew from his deep studies of Ancient Norume the high technology they achieved. After the fall of Norumian civilization, when the ignorant barbarians took over, certain scholars tried to translate the fragments of engineering manuals that survived. In many instances inventions like the steam engine, the wet cell, and even the telescope, were left out by those who did the copying because they did not understand what it was. This created great holes in Norumian archaeology until the coming of the modern era. Questions baffled scholars from the Pre-Evil times on Amazia how the Norumians achieved the things they did. What is called the passage of time is the historian's reflection on time.

"Even here there are parallels…" mumbled Alack. "Where are the mystery panels, Sir?"

"We have here, at the end, grouped until revelation opens our eyes." They went to the last walls of chiseled writing. Alack opened his Calcomp and brought up his images, making sure he had them all.

"Can I see the Vault of Jars you speak of?"

That's even older than this…come."

He followed the Hishtar as they seemed to meander down very old parts of the temple complex. Buildings of incredible antiquity, whose architecture is totally different from other sections, are great heaps of ruins. All the upper structures are piles of fallen masonry. Gigantic cut slabs of stone tumbled about like a giant's discarded set of toys building blocks. Everything is covered in sprawling creepers of a tree-like algae plant, upending and toppling the walls and minaret's. But the lower halls and vaults are still intact. Swept clean by the priests, they led on towards the inners of a worn mountain that is now only a hill. Some walls have been carved with high base reliefs of strange images of triangular bodies with elaborate headgear. Others are symbols and writings not of the Ancient Venusian style.

"Sir, these letters and carvings aren't Amtorian?"

"We don't know them, only others, please follow."

Alack made digitals of everything with his low light settings. An ancient, musty feeling assailed him. Something so old it is lost in the primordial depths of the soul, only a dim spark is a remnant from a DNA gene long since turned off or neglected. Getting a telltale feeling he is the first to see this and felt a spasm of excitement. The stale, drafty air became a tonic, uplifting his inners to new levels. Something dormant began to stir and rattle his discipline. As they trudged deeper into the subterranean past, Alack's heart began to race. A damp sweat broke his skin, adding to a clammy, contained emotion, as if something very old wanted to escape but it cannot. It stretched and squeezed, making his tensile flesh bend and buckle. He wanted to speak, but his vocal cords tightened, and twisting in the lower throat made him change his mind. The base reliefs became harsher in the yellow torchlight, adding further to the dismal mood of the arching downward tunnel. Something about the images changed. The weird triangular bodies are in violent poses. Strange snake like appendages arched out, striking an oval of darkness. The ovals became heaps, piled about their crooked feet. Some form of combat, but of a non-humanoid nature. Things not recognizable by a sane mind danced and pranced in a weird ritual slaughter.

"The Chamber of Jars..." intoned the Little Priest as he yanked a lever and a great stone door rolled open with ease. "Tread carefully and give a prayer for those whose energy is no longer amongst us." Alack noticed there are three other stone doors with curved symbols splattered in various indiscernible forms. About to comment, the Hishtar activated a modern lighting panel. Behold, Chamber of Jars!"

Stretching even deeper into the chasm of gloom is a vaulted tunnel. Carved by some none mechanical means, it held many shelves of the same rock material along the walls. On the shelves are round, oblong jars of a heavy, dark, stone-like substance. A single symbol, a curved line with a round oval, is imprinted on each jar. Alack took readings, recognizing the symbol from very ancient Norumian temples. One of the old spirits that evolved into the Ufuries the Norumians placed about for good luck.

"Metabar..." mumbled Alack studying his distorted readings over the error messages, "These jars are made of one of the hardest substances known...and the most durable." Making further adjustments, he gasped, forcing out his voice. "They're so old even my device can't give me an age..." Without thinking, he sent a psychic finger out and it shot back causing a slight headache. Anything stronger, and the rebound would hurt.

"These Jars go back before life began." The Priest pointed his staff towards a wall section where a hole was made and repaired. The cement and bricks used did not match the original materials. "They came to plunder here…" He gestured to an opposite wall with empty shelves and broken jars scattered on the floor. From the thousands stretching off into the gloom, about a hundred are missing. "Pray for lost spirits stolen from holy places. Pray for the children of forgotten ages. Pray they find peace in another life."

Alack fingered the broken fragment of metabar noticing something inside had been taken. He scanned the pieces and then began sweeping all the shards in a frenzy. "Whatever was taken no longer causes distortions…metabar has a unique quality, when broken, the crystalline structure can be dated from the impact." Going down on all fours, Alack scurried about like a canine looking for a treat. "How metabar is made is a mystery…" His round athletic ass shot back and forth. "We think the Krill used the nuclear fission fusion of a star's core to mold it…" Alack's hair bounced as he crawled in and out of places. "It is the hardest substance known…" Banging his head on the repaired wall section stopped. "This is recent…" Finishing, Alack stood glaring down at the Priest. "Some of these pieces are sixty years old, and others are less and less up to modern times. When were you last in here?"

"It my predecessor who discovered the hole sixty years ago. Before, no one has never been here, only last Shuton of Amtor, and he left a pile of dead Mistugogi afterwards."

"The last governor of Amtor from Unapiteria was in here?"

"His Palasatro, after evacuation, defiled the sacred Chamber and was made holy by blood of our ancient brethren. We cleaned and deified bones, sealing off sacred places until we heard noises in the hills."

"Noises?"

"Digging noises. We thought the Nefasta (spirits) had returned, but demons are of flesh and blood uses strong hands to steal. My predecessor discovered thievery going on and sealed the chamber forever."

Alack ran some dating numeric programs on the shards, creating charts, frowning. "By these pieces this has been going on for a long time. The oldest broken piece is about sixty years ago and the most recent is about five. As you stated…before that, did they dig through the hill?"

"We found the airshaft enlarged by efforts. It has since been sealed."

"That explains the air. So, whoever has been breaking these jars and taking whatever is inside has been doing it on and off…also, Sir, the missing jars on the shelves don't add up to the volume of debris on the floor. I think other Shutons came in here and took a few…" Alack's mumble even disturbed him. "What is in these jars and those in the other three chambers?"

"Remains of the Villars."

"You mean those depicted on the walls outside?"

"It's what we think."

Alack came up closer and glared down at the Priest. "Do you realize what you're saying, Sir? In these funeral urns are the pieces of the Great Krill, a race that existed half a million years ago!"

"In a sacred place, time does not exist." The Hishtar turned towards the door. "We spent too long with the dead, let's return to living." After sealing everything Alack followed the little stubby Priest to the open air of the temple complex, and, for the first time, felt relief breathing in the natural heavy humidity.

That evening, back in his room at the quaint inn, Alack sat cross-leg on the thick rug in the main room studying his Calcomp. Those nimble fingers dashed over the keyboard; others moved icons on the screen at lightning speeds. His mind, burning and swirling, a typhoon of thoughts and concepts, fought in desperate waves to get an answer. After a good hour of painful mental gymnastics Alack caught the whip and found his target. He made a quick comparison of the distortion error messages from the Demon Stone in the jewelry shop at Newlon City to those of the unbroken urns.

They are identical!

'The same energy caused the error messages…which means those jars hold the Nex Astorum crystals. Is it possible that Hishtar is right, those things are the remains of the Great Krill?' His eyes went to a piece of the gray hard metabar shard he stole. 'And how did they break these?' Alack shot to his bare feet and began pacing at a feverish pace. His long locks bounced like a rolling sea. 'We know so little about them…the people they brought from other worlds to attend the gardens around their cities never saw their masters. Those stone reliefs in that tunnel are the only images…and I saw them! Meander where are you when I need you the most!' Alack swore in native Seminian over the fact that Amtor does not fully have a Cosmic Net. He cannot send his images to the archeologist's website from his Calcomp. Pausing, Alack mumbled, recalling an old proverb from his home world. "Great souls do not perish with the body…"

Feeling suddenly hot, he felt a burning down below, realized he was ravenous.

Alack's hunger is so deep and driving that he forgot about his 'expander' pills and ran downstairs in his black sleeping shorts.

"Feed me!" He pounded the table, almost breaking the hemp and cloth surface.

The funny bell-shaped head of hair Waiter with a sour expression took the huge order and within several minutes, Amtorian dish after dish met it's demise. Alack's gut knew no limit. He inhaled things he would never try, even a huge stuffed Amtorian Rat! Eventually, after the last leafy, tasty nut dessert salad, Alack is full. From the kitchen, they stared at him. That huge mound of lifeless muscles was hunched up, eyes closed, silent, still, and digesting. The little Amtorians wondered if they should run away or go out and get more provisions, but a loud, satisfying 'burp' erupted from the corner table. They smiled and began chatting amongst themselves.

A thought exploded in Alack's head.

Now that his mind is clear, those base reliefs on the walls of the jar chamber came alive. Something inside of him stirred. Some deep feeling, long since interred, broke from the surface and presented itself. Those carvings are more than just pictures. Alack must go back and study them further. He must try a new method for revelation.

Paying the bill, he dashed to his room, got dressed, grabbed his Calcomp and ran out into the street of the little village. Sneaking his way into the temple, avoiding the Mistugogis, arrived behind the complex at the ruins, and went down to the first panel. 'There's something not right about these…' he thought about doing another scan, but a deeper one. The Calcomp is modified to be a high-end device. When Octor Lambert was alive, he and Alack added applications and devices not of the normal for his field work. But after several different quanta level scans revealed nothing. In a moment of frustration, Alack tried his new idea. He sent his mind out in anger, and it bounced back, giving him a bad headache. The same he got when he tried to sweep the Demon Stone in the jewelry store and the unbroken jars in the vault.

Realizing his error, Alack fell to the floor and took a lotus position.

Relaxing, he first drove away the headache and then put himself into a meditative mode. Reaching his normal level for deep metaphysical rejuvenation, which he does for his mind the way he keeps his body fit, he prepared another mental sweep. This one is gentle, a gossamer finger, dainty wavering over the surface of the stone. As if a soft cotton ball swab graced the cold material, he felt it. Lines of force vibrated; a strange ocean like the tumbling of an ancient undertow. Gentle and serene, it carried him along like a tiny, refreshing breeze.

Alack carefully withdrew his gentle touch. 'There's energy here…implanted energy…of course! How stupid can I be! The Great Krill in their final centuries were a telepathic race, all of these images have implanted mental energy patterns, but my mind isn't strong enough to turn them on and learn their message. But, maybe, my subconscious mind is!' Now knowing the access key, Alack put himself into a deeper meditative sleep, 'dreams…'

The sensation of forced slumber, which he does on long spatial trips, felt like a downward plunge into some infinite fantasy. But something resonated around, a weird vibration of string energy snippets sent his subconscious mind unraveling the simmering colorful lines on the high base reliefs. Catching a certain application flow of psychic energy opened a door that has been shut for over five thousand centuries. As a series of triangular vibrating passageways imposed themselves on another, Alack's thoughts came fast and furious in dreamlike waves. A crazy overlapping of non-Euclidean shapes and sizes swept passed his mind's eye in ever increasing meanings.

'My mind went down through the eons of the past! The ages of time ascended backwards, as if a stairway slid beneath without end, a spiraling into the very essences of some forgotten landscape long since abandoned by logistics. The shadowy features of dead eons are a wonder and darkness at the same time. A twisting of images not similar to this world or our sciences swirled around me in a cosmic dance. My inner eye beheld the changing world, of sheets of stars, the dying of stellar hosts, and the birth of hatcheries, all at speeds no one can comprehend. I came upon an age steeped in mystery and horror, a falling away of our values, of human sanity that collapsed in the womb of lost time. There rushed upon me a terrifying ordeal stripping my crude senses bare.'

Alack witnessed some form of combat between the coldness of the triangular entities and the darkness within an oval shape; a ritual slaughter of one race against another, to a purging covering worlds and stars without names or numbers. Amongst the Black Ovals, a deadly and daring plan is hatched before all succumb to extinction. Some special corps of Ovals, five thousand strong, trained to die and save their racial remnants, are scattered. Crystals, the demon stones of death, are made within the bowels of these shapeless Ovals of blackness. But the triangular conquerors learn of the plot. They are gathered in a great place and slaughtered to the last; a black day for a dying race. The gems within their bodies were removed and in-housed in a new material made from the ash of the black dwarf. The thousands of jars are interred for all eternity…

A series of noises quickly brought Alack from his deep mental sleep.

The hairs at the nape of his neck rang like a battle klaxon.

Twelve small Amtorians, in skimpy straps holding various martial arts weapons, glared at him at eye level as he sat on the cold floor. Dapo, holding a sack with some weighty thing in it, raised his bell-shaped sour face, "you hear and why? Get going and out before we attack. You still messed up!"

Alack, revived and ready, counted heads and saw their weapons, spiked his metabolic rate. With this new knowledge, he suddenly grasped their intentions. Spreading his knotting legs in a split angled his body for their onslaught. "So, it's you and your guys who have been looting this place. I advise you to cease and go home, Dapo, or I'll have the Eparch arrest you all." Alack's mind in overdrive quickly calculated his next dozen moves in advance.

Those recessed eyes went wide as the sour face became a gruesome mask of hostility. "Sorry to do this, you know things you should not." In a funny clicking of fingers, they crouched and attacked.

Alack inhaled, placing his palms on the hard stone floor, and lashed out in flare work.

Gyrating in swinging cycles, his powerful legs struck with terrible force. Boot heels, hard and deadly, smacked ugly, sour faces, sending bodies crashing against the walls. In some swings, both his legs act as one powerful wrecking ball, in other gyrations, single legs crashed into the agitated heads. Constantly moving with flare and finger work back and forth, they tried to hit and stab him, but his speed is unreal. Within minutes, more than half of the attacking force is out cold and disarmed.

As the remaining four charged with ball and chain weapons, Alack spun to a handstand. Leaping up, felt the curvature of the walls and ceiling, and slid down behind them. Lashing out with his fists, fell to his knees, and rolled. As he spun on his back and sides, more leg kicks took out the others; their silly weapons clanging away in the darkness of the tunnel. Jumping to his feet, Alack faced glaring down at Dapo, who was clutching the sack.

"Now, Dapo, we can talk. What weapon do you have there?"

"The thing I cut your knee caps off!" In one quick move, the little Amtorian whipped out a big pair of heavy calipers and tried to snag Alack's lower legs. In one quick swipe, faster than a bolt of lightning, tore the device from his grasp. Another swipe and Dapo is airborne, crashing into the back wall. Falling down to a crumpled position on the floor, Dapo did not move.

Powering down his raging heart, Alack examined the heavy metallic calipers. The inside edges held sparkling gems like diamonds, big and well placed on both inner sides of the curved arms. At the axel junction is a spring mechanism with handles and a crank. A series of corresponding lines and knobs controlled an inner electronic device. Strange scroll writing adorned all the free surfaces. An idea entered his head after a quick examination. "So, this is how they broke the jars…some type of crystal vibration…a valuable leftover from the Krill!"

T. A. Elanus, Director General of the Amazian Special Services, pondered through Alack's field report correcting grammar and spelling. This annoying long de-briefing procedure follows the conclusion of every assignment or Affair issued to him since the beginning. Still, he found it tiresome, irritating, and unsettling as the 'old man' tore apart his analysis the way he does with a hefty slab of cooked meat. But T. A.'s facial expressions under the prancing bangs of gray hair are different. That caustic, twisting frown, which Alack has seen so often, is not there. A weird puckering of the lips and cheeks made him unreal, not the Boss he recognized.

"This is so fantastic it's absurd!" He tossed the data reader back at Alack, who caught it without any effort. "I want a proper field report, not an antiquarian fantasy."

Alack carefully stood up and placed it back so as not to damage the electronics. "It's all true Sir. You yourself have told me I'm not imaginative enough to make this stuff up. I followed your orders. I discovered the source. I went to Amtor to investigate and stopped the agency that has been distributing the Demon Stones to potentates of other worlds. End of the Affair and the line, Sir!" Alack's smug expression convinced T. A. to go back to his report as he took the seat again. "I dwell not in the past but in the future."

"Alright. The first Unapiterian Shuton of Amtor, Saccromita was seeking plunder to enrich himself and discovered the Monastery and the vaults below. He killed many of the priests until they showed him the jars of metabar. His people found a way to break them and take the Nex Astorum stones. This continued for several centuries until Amtor achieved independence and stopped the plundering. A new generation of priests and Villicus, sponsored by those Amtorian families who served the Shutons, continued secretly over the ages to steal the jars. Eventually, a new group of priests stopped this. But the Amtorian families found a way in and continued to steal a little at a time. Eventually this was stopped and the vaults sealed sixty years ago. Now you come along in your shorts and encounter those who are the descendants seeking to take another haul from the vaults." T. A. made a loud snort. "I can accept this. It's modern, and the timing is believable. Crime and thievery exist in every age. See, I can make a saying too."

"But the other part is not? It goes back more than a million years ago." Alack is up pacing around the chair. "Worshippers of darkness and drinkers of common blood, is how the Great Krill described the Ziates. They found the whole race so disgusting they killed them all off. But we must not forget the Ziates were the first race to evolve on Amazia, the Krill were the invaders. My subconscious unlocking of the energy in the base reliefs showed them as ovals of darkness, no physical form is recorded."

"And the Krill? What did they look like?"

"As we think, short, triangular, no shoulders but arms protruding from chest, their sides down to legs, pointed heads with strange bioelectronics attached, my impression was they were half bio and half machine, something like that, Sir." Alack lost energy and fell back into his chair. "But, not machines as we know mechanics, something totally alien than those on Mystros, from the Day-Zano Affair." His athletic ass painfully yanked something sharp he sat upon.

About to comment, T.A. saw the item. "What's that in the bag?"

"The device they used to break the metabar jars and get the crystals." T. A. clicked his fingers, and Alack removed it placing the calipers on his desk.

"Remarkable, Alack m'boy…remarkable…"

"You can see the seal of Shuton Saccromita, his family, and those who are charged with the use of this device, plus other unknown symbols. I had it translated…it's all in my report." Alack fell back into his seat. "They stole it, hiding it so no one could open the jars."

Elanus fingered the sharp diamonds along the insides of the calipers. "They place the jar in here, clamp it around, and apply pressure with this crank. Very simple?"

"Not so. Not just diamonds, Sir, but an inner device that makes vibrations of sound using the gems as a conduit of force. As you activate it you turn it counter clockwise, like in a screwing manner…"

"Diamonds are not stronger than metabar, but adding in what you said negates the natural conditions." Losing interest, he went back to Alack's handsome face. "You think, or were you told by the latent energy in the carvings, that the crystals in the jars were made by the Ziates themselves, the way a clam makes a pearl or something similar?"

"Yes, Sir. But these were made by a special group to be used against the leaders of the Krill. Somehow, they were to be distributed amongst their leadership causing them to go insane and stop the annihilation of the Ziate race. But the Krill learned of the plot, rounded up all the special conspirators, killed them, and deposited their crystals in jars of metabar, sealed for all time."

"Until Saccromita and his people began selling them to the highest bidder?"

"That's about the size of it, Sir."

"And the Histar Priests, you handed the thieves over to them?" Alack nodded in the affirmative. T. A. leaned back, twirling his thumbs. "What was Amtor like?"

"Not what the travel brochures and digital images show. Few parts of the planet are modern, almost interesting, but a drabness is everywhere. The people are strange, they accept everything as is, why make any changes. A certain lack of desire to improve their lot and seek something different is not there. I've talked to a few scientists, and they give the planet about thirty million years before the inner core becomes dormant. When that happens, the magnetosphere will decline allowing solar winds and flares to stripe away the atmosphere. In about a hundred and fifty million years, Amtor will be like Barsoom, with a thin atmosphere barely able to support life."

"A hundred and fifty million years...?" T.A.'s fixed stare is unnerving as he studied something far beyond Alack's plumage of auburn long hair, "Spinaza said, 'human life is very cheap when money is a motive behind an action.' That is what I understand about all this. That is what concerns me the most than what happened in the very distant past or the very far future. I got this far and this position by practicing the art of practicality and not dreaming of things beyond our self-made reality."

"Didn't the Emperor once say, 'by forgetting the past, you lose continuity with your life for living in the future,' or something like that."

"Smart ass."  Elanus's attention went back to the old caliper device.  "You know, Alack m'boy, this would be good in the Special Service Museum."

Alack frowned.  "We don't have one, Sir…"

"And why not?  The Imperial Control Army has one over at Provida and the SSG has a nice collection in the foyer at the Citadel, why not we start one."

"Sometimes I can't tell when you're serious or joking, Sir."  He stood quickly and grabbed the calipers from the desk.  "That would tell the public we exist, we don't need publicity, and I want this for my little collection."  Alack sat, gave it a pleasing nod and wrapped the bag around it.  "Between the sword from Microsus and the Dramid helmet from Praxis I think it would look nice…"

"You're starting to annoy me.  To end this, we've notified the ICA, the SSG, and the Universal Health Agency of the General Assembly and Space Council.  They will notify all their ambassadors and representatives over the hazards of those Demon Stones.  Since the Amtorian Eparch authorities seized the offenders, and since we have their cracking device, I doubt anymore plundering will take place.  The Eparch wants his stones back."

"I sent my archeological friend Meander a report on my findings."  Alack broke a funny smile, curling the ends of his lips.  He knew this would irritate his Mentor.

"You Venderian!  He will find the vault with the jars, and this nonsense will begin again!"

"Sir, I thought about that. The Arkgalus and his Mistugogi have strict orders to show him only the base reliefs. My report does not mention the funeral chamber, the Ziate crystals, or the jars, only the wall carvings."

"Not even the hidden, engrained energy patterns?"

"Nothing is sacred and nothing of the sort, Sir."

Elanus seemed to relax as a grin stretched his features. "Well, Alack m'boy, there's hope for you after all, in the past and in the present. Now get out!"

THE END

# THE NARGUN-MACARA AFFAIR

By Ernest Velon

The coolness of the mountain air mingled with the heat from the rocks and crags of the Gorge of Validor, making the small enclosed valley a pleasant place to idle in. Above, in starry splendor, the stretched and streaked expanse of Cygnus arm of the Fylight (Milky Way) galaxy added substance to the upper regions of the sky. The titanic gas plume of burning red and stark cold blues heightened the spatial jewels in levels of radiance, as certain blue giants and red dwarfs are able to penetrate the cascading dust from the Rykorian (Fonton) Globular cluster (M29). With all this natural beauty above, a gentle breeze made the Validor a romantic place to spend the night.

Loud and noisy, the dozen terrain vehicles bounced and roared over the rocky trail between the cliffs, sending echoes and much clatter to the nocturnal animals about. Laughter and giggling amongst the two dozen teenagers from the local school made the silence run and hide away. With backpacks and saddle bags, the cavalcade of young, energized guys and girls came to a roaring halt at the black maw of a cave. Two gigantic boulders, with chiseled marks and painted graffiti, worn and almost invisible in the feeble starlight, told their leader this was the place to party.

The Mountain Bivaks (a gymnastic wrestling team) had just won the annual championship games. They squashed their competitors from the lazy city suburbs of the fertile plains with resounding victories. In all routines and weight classes, they crushed and splattered their challenger's sweat all over the mats and apparatus. A twisting, flipping array of headlocks and back scooping made legends from boys to men. A huge conquest ended with bands, rowdy youths marching down the main street of Validor City, and speeches by the Mayor and local Prefect, all ending in a massive victory dance at the local town square.

A great feast followed, and while everyone was diverted, one of the Athlete's broke into his father's store and stole several cases of Brevaziar wine and Hempfola Beer. The main champion, who bested their best, broke down the back door to the local grocery store and, like plundering Judorites took what was required for a nightly orgy under the stars. They came with their girls, a wobbling army of festive bright eyes and chattering tongues, to the Validor Gorge. From behind closed doors and in the empty silence of bedrooms late at night, the legends spoke a sleepless tale of hideous happenings five years ago to frighten unruly children and enjoy the campfire scare before turning in.

Such talk, in the beginning, was squashed as nonsense by the mining Director and even the SSG Prefect joined him in disclaiming such horror as fabricated. Validor City, wiped from the face of Entro-Palis III, a mining town of four hundred, all inhabitances never seen again. The SSG requested assistance, and a Special Service Agent came and poked about the silent, wind-swept homes for about an Amazian week. According to the mining Director it was gas, a potent poisonous heavy cloud of fumes from shaft number four that crawled, spilling and killing everything in its path. A noxious bundle of eroding agents and bacteria, a subterranean bowel release from a time when the planet was soft and malleable, escaped and poured like unseen lethal venom to the town below.

But such talk in bars, around dinner tables, and in bathhouses by the people who the mining Director quickly brought in, found the gas story not fully the truth. Even the Agent fellow from Amazia drew a different scenario along with the local Prefect. Various tidbits of evidence failed to support the Director's ultimate conclusion of what really happened. The absence of hard evidence like bones, tissue, and clothing failed to convince those who could think. Unfortunately, credits talk and incompetence walks, the Director had his day, the gas story was believed, new people and their families arrived, the mining began again, and payroll was issued with bonuses. All is happy again in the Validor mining community of Entro-Palis III.

The teenagers knew the place of horror and were thrilled by the whispering tale.

They came from MaCara eighty years ago, several thousand robust colonists, chartered by the Administration of Planets to develop Entro-Palis III. Located on the edge of the Rykorian cluster in the Regent of Byfilbia, they brought their cattle, factories, and culture, all Amazian based, to plant their new feet in a Class A world. Validor City, named after its founder, Encla Validor, rose from the flat waste to gleaming splendor. By the present day, boasting a population of one million, dozens of new vibrant metropolises tamed a wild planet; or so they thought.

Something hideous crawled from shaft four, now abandoned.

Some obnoxious guests preferred the less social daring scientific tale. Another deeper story whispered and passed about by hidden tongues. Some miner found a strange stone and gave it to his daughter as a gift. She cleaned it with water and placed it on her dresser that night. The water hatched it. From there, the horror began and swept away all humanoid and animal life in the robust mining town. When shipments and communications ceased, the mining Director came with the Prefect and gazed upon an empty heaven of dusty desolation.

From this the legends and horror stories multiplied.

After five years, it still lingered in the minds of the young. A dare, a challenge, a lessening of priorities, a thrill to camp out and party at the very maw of hell itself; and it is here the Mountain Bivaks made their last party camp.

Later in the night, after the fuel for the campfire is exhausted, after empty bottles are strewed over the prickly stones and gravel, after torn bags of snack foods and ripped boxes of take-out meals littered, mixed snoring came from the portable tents. From one big tent came a moaning sound as four legs, one male and one female, rolled and pumped in a hormonal embrace. After a spasm of juices and semen, a warm sweat parted both teenagers. Their breathing returned to normal, the last bottle of wine was emptied without the use of glasses, each delighting in the lustful victory of their young, vibrant flesh. It is the husky, muscular adolescent who began to shake from massive hunger. The girl fell asleep quickly, but he is ravenous.

Driven by some wild food fever, he left the tent, seeking anything to eat amongst the piles of litter. But another just emerged after five years of silent hibernation and found a delicious morsel of throbbing muscles in red splotched underwear.

"You haven't changed…much, Colonel." Mentioned Prefect Gallopus of Validor City too, the tall young man in the tight white short-sleeved polo shirt, black pants, and shiny Service boots. An outdated looking Calcomp strung over a massive upper body, the strap pulling over broad shoulders. With envy, the Prefect took in the tapering thighs and thin waistline where a SSG utility belt almost hung on his hips. A powerful chest and pectorals stretched the white fabric as Gallopus marveled at the youth's physique. He seemed to get better looking while getting flabbier. The long, well-groomed auburn dark hair, parted in the middle tapering down to the collar, where it curled up. He recalled that boyish face, between the chiseled hardness of a man and a maturing adolescent, did not change. Those big brown eyes, heavy lips, all seemed like he was here just yesterday. If he had admired him before, he now fought a desire to worship.

"I came as soon as you called," Alack Troyus of the Special Services held out his ID Card but Gallopus gestured to an empty seat by his desk. "My Boss recalls my last visit five years ago and feels I should personally follow up. This Affair is not closed, Sir, and remains open on the books."

"I didn't know that, Colonel. When you left half a decade ago, there were bad words, bad feelings, and not the usual hospitality of this place, but not from this office. Now, we have the same problem, Colonel, again, I support you, a single voice the others ignored. You are right…" He trailed off in an uncertain mumble.

"The past is full of uncertainties, and two are better than one. I re-read all my data on the Nargun Affair, the books are still open on Entro-Palis III." Alack relaxed in the hard wooden chair, Gallopus was not into soft comfortable furniture, and that is what he recalled the most about this backyard Prefect. "So, returning to my original conclusions, it must be some type of predator from ancient times."

"Damn…by Kranos, it's like you never left!" Gallopus pushed a data disk at the handsome, intense face. "Yes, this time we'll make it stick. But this time the killings are not all at once. If you recall, the entire town's population vanished almost overnight, but now it's limited to a single group." Alack took the crystal and inserted it into his Calcomp bringing up the report. "I thought you would get the new issued upgrade?"

"I had the chance, Sir, but this works fine, with a few of my own improvements."

"Frankly, Colonel, when you walked into my office, I wasn't quite sure it was you." Alack's blink over his screen is a question. "I mean the way you ate the last time you were here, I thought you'd be as fat as a house, and I see you're even better looking than before. How do you do it?"

"I live a simple Seminian lifestyle, Sir." His intense brown eyes continued to read the Prefect's report, keeping his reply simple. "Unlike you, no offense, Sir, your uniform is a little on the heavy side."

"None taken. It's called aging…and the good life."

"So good, it's good for nothing."

"And I haven't forgotten your snide remarks, where's that one from?"

"The Unapiterians…" Alack closed his Calcomp giving

Gallopus direct eye contact. "Definitely the same creature, but we have better DNA samples than the last time. Your digital forensics now proves this. The little girl's last entry in her bedside diary proves the rock found in Shaft Four was some kind of prehistoric egg from your deep past time, the water she used re-animated it to hatch, and the rest is five years ago!"

"It's not good to hold grudges, Colonel. That shit bouncing around in your brain will only make you stumble and fail. All that gas shit from Director Lusitan is corporate-concocted starshit. He isn't going to like this."

"Isn't it Lusiton?"

"You left such a bad taste of Amazia after your last visit he reverted back to the original spelling."

"Fruit and shit go together, he's still with the mining concern?"

"Bigger and worse than ever...I would dare to say we now have two creatures on my planet, Colonel," Alack slumped in the hardback seat, his handsome face taking on a frown as memories poured in. "He isn't going to like you, Colonel. You were a thorn in his ass before, now you're using a pickaxe and crowbar."

"Waste is popular until the bill is paid." a weird gurgling sound filled the simple, quiet office. "I can't think on an empty stomach." He stood, smacking his ripped belly. "Is that nice little eatery still across the street?"

"Yes. And Brama's Luncheonette still has your face scratched on the wall of the only biped who can down two of her Muck Rake steaks."

"Then, I have some catching up to do!"

"I live to eat…" burped Alack into the shocked face of Gallopus as they left the quaint luncheonette, two SSG men took up the rear as they crossed the Silorian (road). "And I think the cooking got better."

The thin face of Gallopus squinted, driving away the image of Alack's unreal intake. "But not your appetite, Colonel. I've forgotten the other time you came here, and, now when I see that eatery, I get sick. A shade of green!" The two Men behind him chuckled.

"If it's good for the septic system, it's good for me. Your town was all pre-fabs and shanty structures, now theirs real buildings besides your Praetorium, Prefect."

"The Royal Reeve (mayor) wanted to attract more miners and workers, so he invested in solid contractors than something that can be torn down and moved."

"Good idea." Alack slapped his belly, another annoying habit. "Now I'm ready to begin, let's go to the camp sight." Gallopus snapped his fingers in the SSG sign language, and the men piled into another black Zo car with the square cross surrounded by a wreath of oak leaves in white and gold. Before Gallopus could comment again on Alack's eating habits, he yanked on his safety belt. "Has anyone been to the murder sight?" This SSG Zo car is the same as the last time, the older model has not yet been replaced.

"I made sure the mortuary guys didn't disturb much…"

"You mean there are actual bio remains?"

"Nothing substantial, just lots of litter and shredded tents, torn backpacks, I just wanted them to be the first for biometric forensics. There's nothing in the mortuary to examine Colonel." Within seconds they are airborne leaving the town behind.

"I thought there were laws when downtown?"

"I don't enforce'em, only if some drunken miner and his juiced up friends abuse their privileges on payday, then they feel my heel." He activated the siren and pulsating lights. "It's official, I like doing this."

"I didn't expect a parade, Prefect."

"I'm announcing the glutton from Amazia is back!"

When they arrived at the Validor Gorge the two vehicles touched down away from the site. Alack is the first leaping over the closed door and whipping out his Calcomp. So swift, his feet touched the dirt as the machine bounced slightly, the Calcomp display in full scanning mode.

"Where's my fregging flags!?" Gallopus snapped his fingers, gesturing in wild sweeps as his two waiting men jumped. "Who cleaned up my site?"

"I thought you said the mortician staff only did their scans? According to your report, there should be litter everywhere and clues..." Alack swung his broad upper body, getting a full reading from the sensor nods. "There's nothing here...someone used a bio-bomb to erase all bacteria, DNA, hair, fingerprints...it's sterile!" Alack's shoulders slumped in annoyance. He saw the two big boulders flanking the entrance to shaft Four. "Even the claw marks I found five years ago are chiseled off..."

"Colonel Troyus, believe me, I gave orders not to disturb this site." In an angry growl, Gallopus yanked open his Portafon (cell phone) and shouted at someone at the other end, then frowned at one of his men. An index finger pointed and waved him over. "Explain this!"

"The Royal Reeve made me do it. He wanted it spick and span...Sir."

"This is a crime scene, not your mother's kitchen!" Gallopus fumed, facing Alack. "Our Mayor has a fetish for cleanliness…that buffoon! He thinks he's doing good, everything he touches turns into a cursed mess. What would they do with an idiot on Amazia?"

"The Emperor would probably send him away as ambassador to a place nobody has ever heard of."

"I like that, a place so far no one knows it exists."

"Didn't he know twenty-four young people died here?"

"Including his daughter…yes, she was part of that group." Gallopus gave a loud snort, rubbing his nose. "I'm sorry, Colonel, I thought I had some answers after five years."

Not allowing frustration to sap his determination, Alack swung around, heading to the open maw of the mind's shaft. A sign warning visitor not to enter had graffiti painted in ancient MaCarian, 'Shy'zik atra Kranos'. Alack scanned it using his translator software, "there is no hope in Hell'. Not bad…has this been checked out?"

"If you recall, Colonel the Sylak people closed shaft Four after the town was destroyed. They claimed the deadly gas came from here."

"Why don't we go and see…"

"I think not. You can go only a few hundred Illos in and the rest is underwater. The shaft continues until it ends abruptly, then plunges a Sectal (almost a mile) down to lower shafts. The natural springs have filled it up since they removed the pumps."

A loud exhale as those broad shoulders slumped further. "Let's go see your mortician, Prefect." A creeping feeling of depression began to return. The same confined nausea Alack had five years ago from this place. He hated the frustration of going no where's, of achieving nothing substantial.

A shanty of a shed next to the town's hospital held the stasis chambers and other instruments the mortician used. The man was not here, he left his assistant in charge. Not very helpful until Alack mentioned what happened to the litter at the sight, and then he showed them several garbage bags out back.

Within minutes, Alack had all the sacks torn open and everything spread out on the back lot. Empty bottles, ripped snack bags, plastic utensils, paper food pouches, and lots of shredded camping fabrics from the tents and clothing, Alack carefully examined everything. When done studied the readouts on the Calcomps screen. Prefect Gallopus waited with his two men and, not wanting to dirty his hands, came forward asking. "Talk to me, Colonel?"

"Lots of sexual activity…male semen and female pubic hair on some of these blankets…I'll send you their DNA signature so you can make positive IDs… saliva…finger prints…even facial hairs…yes…quite a wild time under the stars."

"These are…or were…high powered athletes, our young men, and women, the best Validor City can spit out. Despite their private activities, each one was an honor student."

"Honor?  I doubt it, Sir."  He kicked a pile of torn paper wrappers, "no respect for the plant, that's not honor but stupid, lazy neglect. Didn't anyone teach them not to litter?" Alack finished sending his finds to the Prefect's Affair and came forward facing him. "Students? Yes, still practicing their undercover gymnastics. The best of Validor, my God would disagree and her priests would have a serious talk with the parents. I'm not a slave to convenience."

"Are you a man between the legs, Colonel or someone with shallow muscles? They're all gone and dead, have some remorse, damn it!" Gallopus snorted, trying to be professional. "Only the terrain vehicles remain untouched…" he mumbled.

"That's next on my list." Alack glanced at the mess in the backyard of the mortuary shed. "You can call your mayor to clean this up. The dirtiest jobs are the best ones to do. But I found this wrapped in the torn cloth of a tent." Alack held up a small digital camera. He hot-wired it to his photo imager on the Calcomp and brought up a series of pictures. Lots of young smiling faces, a campfire setting, one guy eating then vomiting and going back for more, a drunken dance between two couples shedding clothes, others falling down laughing, it all ending in a tent interior shot. Two naked bodies between sleeping mats, much heavy breathing and pumping of limbs, then a long moan of a pause, and the youthful, handsome face smiled at the wide shot. In a beastie grin of male conquest, he pumped his fist up and down in a victory sign.

"That's Fremison," grinned Gallopus, "He's the reigning all-around champ and works in the local grocery store for his father. The girl is Ilinda, a local flirt, acrobatic leader of the cheering girls…"

As the others grinned, making obscene sounds, there was a sudden movement of the tent.

Something long, dark and hideous with yellow fangs and a deafening roar of bile swept aside the image, the tent, and both young people are gone in a hazy burst. A tumbling of tearing fabrics and the hindquarters of hairy flailing pods vanished as the camera slipped into the shredded folds.

"Run that again, Colonel!" They witnessed the horrible digital video again. "You've been right all along. I think we found our creature. After five years here's the evidence I can shove up Lusitan's ass!" Gallopus snapped his fingers at his men. "Search every morsel of garbage for digital cameras, and that's an order!" After Alack returned from examining the six terrain scooters and saddlebags, he found the Prefect gloating with hands on hips. Three surviving digital cameras are on a work table tied into his Calcomp. "Look'y here, Colonel, more proof." As he played with various images of the camp sight, young drunken couples making funny faces and sexual groin gestures, something black with a strange glistening texture moved rapidly in the background. So quickly it pounced that within a matter of minutes, the sight is a shambles and flattened.

"Have you tried to get a clear shot of that?"

"No, Colonel…even with enhancers slowing it down, it moves so fast in the dark, this is it." Alack hotwired the file into his Calcomp. "I didn't give you permission!"

"I didn't ask, thanks Prefect," Alack broke a smug grin. "But I have applications that will. We need to confront Director Lusitan with this new evidence."

"As I said, he's pretty big in the corporate levels today."

"But he has to listen, we've got solid proof."

"When I say he's big, I mean really big…" Gallopus extended his arms in a barrel gesture while puffing up his cheeks. "Like dirigible size…humongously fat."

Alack paused, shifting mental gears. "Five years for a Seminian is a long time but for your kind, it is not too long, I remember the Director, he was young and pretty fit looking."

"A lot can happen to even us in half a decade, Colonel. Lucky Lusitan has gotten so heavy he needs a robotic cart to get around. We went to school together at Marinor City, and he was into all the sports and the girls, the most likely to succeed, if you get my stellar drift. Once he got settled in corporate bullshit he just exploded like a red giant. That's why they call him Lucky Lusitan…he's lucky to be alive at six hundred Gross (pounds). He's got a whole staff of servants he's so high up on his ladder."

"Then I think it's time to knock off some of the rungs, Prefect."

"If he falls the hole will be so big and deep, they'll never find him."

Alack grinned, making a smart remark, "Anything a person does is a clue to their character." Alack liked this backyard Prefect.

Yes, Gallopus also forgot how annoying this Special Agent can be.

They arrived at Marinor City, the northern regional capital for the Sylak Mining District of Entro-Palis III. A bustling metropolis of one hundred thousand on the Sylatic Plains at the foot of the Sylak Mountain chain, the tallest skyscraper dominated the center plaza of Marinor. Alack never stopped to change into his formal uniform. So animated he insisted on going to see Director Lusitan right now. His first encounter with this self-made asshole was not very nice. But Alack, always the seeker for competition, wanted another verbal round after five years of festering frustrations. He knew they were being observed by the Mining Company of Sylak and Milston, who else convinced the Mayor of Validor to clean up the site and hide all evidence of the truth. Alack expected Lusitan to receive them without an appointment, and that is exactly what happened.

"I remember you, Colonel Noriis…" It came from behind a huge, ornate desk that swung aside on wheels. Larger than a Zo truck and just as formidable, Lusitan, in a robotic chair with hydraulic legs and arms, rumbled towards them. Dressed in black wrap-around sarongs, he resembled a grotesque spider from Rozian V. Gallopus is right, his arms and legs are mere stubs. How can a humanoid get like this in only five years?

"It's Colonel Alack Troyus, Special Services." Alack concealed the shock on his face with a grin. He held up his identification card.

"I've seen that once and I never forget, so put that away, Colonel, your forgetting, we're old friends." As the black mass buzzed lumbering at them Alack heard the carpeted floor groan beneath. "Prefect, how's the family doing?"

"All is well and happy, Director. Do you know why we're here?"

"Not the slightest, but do go on and on and on…" he giggled, the massive torso rumbling like a tank of jelly.

Alack scanned the fleshy face with a tiny gossamer finger of his mind and felt the concealment of truths. He intends to play silly games with us.

"Remember the Gas Murders at Validor City five years ago? Well, to put a Meo in a cage, it's started again in the Validor Gorge. Two dozen high school adolescents vanished from a camp site without a trace." He held out the data disc. The recessed greasy eyes and ponderous whitewashed features with compacted makeup hesitated.

'He knows,' thought Alack working on a strategy to outfox him.

'One sin is as bad as another.'

"Such a shame, me and some of my friends, all one hundred and four, are seriously thinking of having an old fashioned cookout at that very spot. Now you tell me the flesh-eating gas microbes are back in force? I'll send another team to eliminate them. I'm sure we have some of the spray left somewhere."

"We have proof, Director it's a subterranean creature, the same that wasted the town of Validor five years ago. It has returned and taken the two dozen lives of our best."

A bulging, painful twist of fat creased Lusitan's forehead. "Oh…such pain in hearing that, plus the recollection of last time's annoying verbal tirade. Tish tish Colonel for spoiling my day. A bucket of plaques upon your pretty well-fit body…my my, you've gotten better looking while I became a bloated sort of a whale fellow. Shame on you for maintaining such a fine torso, Colonel, you do us all in, surely a whale of a tale for me."

"This is serious, Director Lusitan." Gallopus jabbed the data crystal at him. "One of the teenagers killed is the daughter of the Reeve of Validor."

"That villainous Reeve! To shame and more shame, I never liked him, he was too simple and obliging, takes his work seriously…oh my stars, leave your damn crystal with my secretary, she'll do the reading and hard copy, now go, I'm a busy man." His robotic seat spun around in a circle as he flapped those tiny arms and legs going back to his desk. "My days are a lonely lot, filled with the mundane, any upsetting is a headache, now go!"

"One other point, Director," spoke up Alack puffing his chest in anger stretching the fabric of the white polo shirt, "I insist you cancel your outing Sir, until this monster is eliminated." Why he recommended that Alack regretted, and kicked himself in the posterior.

"Pooh pooh pooh on you, Colonel Noriis, I'll take it under advisement, and don't do that again, it annoys me, makes me recall the way I once was…so long ago…" As the desk swung engulfing him sensor nodes returned to the implants in his cranium.

The short meeting is terminated.

Once outside, deep in the forested plaza surrounding the corporate tower, Alack halted Gallopus with a rock-hard palm on the Prefect's chest. "I know how to mess him up…that party he's planning must not take place. You must get a list of the guests and contact them they are in great danger. Can you do that?"

Gallopus, who frowned in thought over the flabby, horrific sight, quickly answered. "Uh…yes, your right, that must be stopped before more are killed. I know an assistant secretary who works under his chief one, she's helped me in the past and owes me another favor, time to call in my Duddi chips." A gurgling sound exploded from Alack's slim waistline. He started making funny, painful squints while pulling on the soft fabric of his shirt where his stomach is. "You can't be serious…what we just saw, I won't eat for a full week."

"Animals and stars don't move at the same pace…I'm ravenous! Depression does this to me! That diner over there is in a straight line. Are you coming, I hate to eat alone in a strange place?"

"I'll just have a drink and look the other way, Colonel Noriis."

"You're not funny…" and the quivering mass of muscles ran in a straight line.

Prefect Gallopus had to wait outside rather than watch the young Seminian gluttonize himself into an early grave, so he thought. Lusitan must have done the same, but this guy never gets fat. He suddenly recalled what the Colonel told him, he burns three times the calories of a normal humanoid and can never get full, a two-legged stomach. It was the call on his portafon (cell phone) that shattered his train of thought and forced him back into the simple streetside eatery. "Colonel, there's been another series of vanishing murders, com'on."

A small fleet of SSG Zo's and other Tri-R emergency vehicles filled a small suburban street of pre-fabricated houses, creating a neat array of domestic tranquility. A slightly upper middle-class neighborhood of mining supervisors and third-class engineers lived in pretty decent housing in a quiet environment. Blocked off, the ten quaint one-story houses with gardens in the rear and shrubs in the front became a morass of investigators. At the curb, pulled over to the side, is a long blue and red school Zo bus and a frantic driver.

"As I told your guys, I stopped at every house to pick up a child at the right time in the morning and none came out. After the third house, I began knocking on doors and all of them are empty, the children and parents gone..."

"How often did you make this stop?" asked the interviewing SSG Policeman.

"Everyday at zero nine hundred, the neighborhood association pays me to take their children to the pre-school and take them home..."

"We have a list of all the children and parents, Prefect. We have twenty adults and twenty-five children. Ages four to six, and the parents between twenty-four and thirty-two, plus health records and biometrics for both, all missing."

Alack turned about, activated his Calcomp, and began crawling all over the first house. His relentless drive burned a trail to the next and the next, an obsession to find the missing pieces to his rambling puzzle. Into the cellars, wiggling out a basement window, to the backyard garden and lawn sheds, back to the interior, and even crawled out on the slanted roof. Gallopus held his breath as the lithe black pants and a white shirt leaped to the next roof. A round athletic posterior opened an attic dormer and into another house he went. After a good hour and a half, that handsome body and face came trotting back to the Prefect and his men. The knees of his pants are worn and torn, ripped holes in the polo shirt revealed a rib and muscle, the flock of auburn hair messed and frazzled, but a look of euphoria washed the bright face. The young man is in his element.

Chewing on some type of gum, Gallopus studied the muscular figure. "What did you find that my men already know?"

"The creature was here…last night" he displayed the sensor stats on the Calcomp's screen. "It came in through the back doors and consumed all these people and their offspring…its DNA is all over…"

"You mean ate!" corrected one of the Aides horrified.

"This 'thing' somehow devours its prey with very little blood or body remains, and at every crime scene there's a slight dampness where it killed. I think it doesn't have saliva glands but relies on local sources of water to wash and eat. I also think it accumulates its prey, finds a place with a water source and eats there."

"Then how do you explain the school bus?"

"It must have watched from a distance, saw a quick meal and waited to strike…"

"You make it sound like It's intelligent, Colonel."

"It is, Prefect.  In a predator's way of stalking and hunting it's very smart.  Deep DNA scans show this creature is aquatic, it came from an ocean environment."

"This area was under water millions of years ago, Sir." piped up one of the Aides.  "I've done some prospecting and studied the…"

"That's enough Sergeant," snapped Gallopus yanking his face cheeks in thought, "ancient legends and myths speak of a sea monster called a Macara, some terrible brute that attacked from the shallow waters and sucked away its victims, but that's more northern than southern lore."

"Could be a descendant of our prehistoric monster, have one of your men research it.  I want to speak to anyone from the University about Entro-Palis's deep past.  What happened here makes it paramount that Director Lusitan doesn't have his party."

"While you were crawling on your hands and knees Colonel, I got the list of his party goers.  But this makes no sense, almost all these people are business and social associates who don't like him, and yet he's inviting them to this outdoor jamboree?"

Alack's handsome features broke a strained look, then a quick devilish grin.  "Why that Vendearian…of course…how else would you get rid of your enemies.  Make up some story of burying the hatchet by inviting them to a place where they'll never come back from…ingenious!  If a person lies, they are worse than a thief."

Gallopus started to laugh.  A weird donkey baying that caught the attention of all his men. "I can't believe his craftiness. He's doing it again…"

"Doing what again?" asked Alack giving eye contact.

"When he was going to business school, he had a regular assembly line of females in one door and out the other every day of the week. But one lady wanted to snag him and became pregnant. Her father was wealthy and insisted on a marriage. Realizing that would destroy his life style had his lawyer declare the DNA machine used by the court was not calibrated correctly, and the judge held off until it was fixed. He got hold of male semen from the jockstrap of a fellow athlete and somehow used that when the machine was recalibrated. His friend had to marry the girl, and he walked free as a flying Malaboss. He's done that several times, even to those who claimed him as a friend."

"I've heard about that," giggled another Aide, "they still talk about it in…"

"Enough, Corporal." Gallopus exhaled, glancing at Alack, he hates to be upstaged. "He's crafty and devious, Lucky Lusitan has other meanings."

"We must stop this before more are killed." Insisted Alack as his belly turned. "Start calling those people!"

But they are too late.

Director Lusitan acted swiftly. He found the under secretary who was feeding information to the Prefect, and got rid of her. Using a corporate promotion as a disguise, he sent her to a corporate office on the other side of the planet. Before Gallopus could get his men to make the calls, Lusitan held his party that night. The Validor Gorge was ablaze with campfires, tents, laughter, and much merriment. A huge open animal roast with a line of smiling cooks served out the portions to the delighted patrons. The open Barbot poured and jiggled his alcoholic magic into potions and shots without restraint. If they hated Lusitan before, they have now sampled his hospitality and took on a different opinion of a reformed scoundrel.

Lusitan showed up around midnight and received adulation from those who once hated him. He buzzed about in his mechanical chair with the following Aides smiling and congratulating everyone. He displayed a remarkable memory, knowing all their wives and children, their hobbies, interests, and aspirations. He made promises he will never keep, and as he bantered with the wives and patted the children on their heads, chuckled away malevolently inside that massive fleshy bubbler.

When he felt he had won them all over, he left quietly.

The long, winding road along the Skylar Escarpment tapered down from the mountain chain to the open plains below. Under the brilliant starlight the right side held dark bluish gray ascending cliffs, on the left the open plains of Sylatic. A bright, sparkling dome of lights and steady illumination creased the horizon as Marinor City lit up the distant obscurity. Her needles and beacons took away the gloom as Lusitan and his three men made the slow decline to his waiting Zo limousine.

Feeling refreshed and delighted with himself for such a dastardly plan, he felt this is the starting point of even bigger ambitions and greater corpulence. He has fooled them all! He has risen to the top of his division by riding the backs of friends and foes alike. He has proven his cunning without making mistakes. He has been crafty to turn a bad situation around for his own good. They tried to sue him, to steal from him, to indict him, too bad mouth him, to cause him to fumble, but after tonight all those attempts will be gone forever. A new road and ambitions waits!

'Yes! It's all about me!' He chuckled silently.

As Lusitan removed bottles of expensive wine to give to his three Aides, the dark mass just ahead began to move up at them. 'Good,' he thought, 'that stupid chauffeur is making my trip less painful.' It was not his limousine they encountered but something far worse.

They found the mangled robotic chair in a ditch by the descending road. The sleek white and silvery deluxe Zo Ranger limo was empty, the door was torn off, and shredded driver's seat was ripped asunder.

"This all happened last night," began Prefect Gallopus to Alack as his men crawled all over the site seeking clues. "The same at the Gorge, a shambles of litter but no bodies, just fragments of their DNA and It's."

One of the Aides wearing bio-gloves handed a bottle of wine with green dried streaks all over it. "We found this Sir, and here's our digital forensic scans," the man sent the police analysis to the Prefect's Affair site. "More data is still coming in, Sir."

Alack, who was studying the Zo, then the crumpled chair, came over examining the new finds on his Calcomp. "I think we can locate it, Prefect Gallopus. We now have It's raw DNA in quantity."

Gallopus noticed the Seminian wearing a new set of the same clothes he had on the other day. 'Nothing changes with this guy,' he thought. "You're holding back, talk to me, Colonel?"

"Something's been bothering me about this entire Affair. In all predators, they either strip their kill on the spot leaving a mess of evidence, or digest it in their stomachs until the indigestible pieces build up and they vomit everything in one pile.  Whatever original DNA there is smothered in the same mucus that bottle is covered in."  Alack came forward and faced Gallopus.  "We need to do a bio-LiDAR scan of this area.  If it's not shaft four, I think we'll find It's lair and predict where it is."

"I will say this, Lusitan has or had a fine taste for wines.  That's the best piece of advice I've heard as of yet!  I'll call the Geological Society at Marinor University, I think they have the equipment for that."

"This Macara creature has eaten one hundred and eighty five people, that ejected bottle tells me It's reached it's capacity.  When it vomits all the accumulated remains, it'll start killing again.  If we can locate the place, I think we can get your monster."

"Our monster, Colonel, you're as much involved as I am."  Gallopus handed the evidence back to his Aide.  "Now for the billion-credit question, when we find it how do we kill it?"  Alack paused.  His mouth hung open for a second.  "That's the first time I've seen your white teeth without something going in, Colonel."

"Yes, I've been wondering…but we now have sufficient DNA to make a toxic serum."

"A chemical poison?  That can take Agels."  Gallopus slapped his sidearm on his belt.  "I guess we do it the old fashion and quick way?"

Another SSG Aide brought two people in the black and blue white trim gowns and funny puffy hats of the academic community.  "Colonel Troyus, these fellows are Brilliantines from Marinor

University answering your request.  I brought them right away, Sir."

"Hold the ass crap, Kranos!  This is my investigation," began Gallopus, "I never approved of this."

"A positive thought is a positive way."  Alack exhaled feeling that speed and timing are critical.  "I requested some research from the paleontology labs, hoping to get a better background on OUR monster."

"I wouldn't call the Petio-Balarous a monster, Citizen Troyus. The Skylar and Sylatic Plains are the bottom of an ancient inland sea where its kind lived and spawned.  We've found fossil evidence going back fifty million years until the sea dried up."

"Why?" asked Gallopus, hands on hips, in an arrogant tone.

"Why What, Prefect?"

"Why did the sea vanish!"

"Oh..." the funny, sourer faced Fellow glanced at his partner. "That's your study, Argan."

"Thank you, Tellor.  Geology, it's called geology.  The ground began to rise as the Validor mountain chain began to form.  Entro-Palis has an active core, which gives it healthy magnetosphere and tectonics. The Sea of Skylar drained off leaving its sustenance in the fjords and inlets along the coast.  The egg the small child found still had the germ of life.  Now, it's your area of expertise, Tellor."

"Thank you, Argan..."

"Just tell us where the fregging thing came from!" shouted Gallopus losing it.

"Well!  You can't hurry millions of years into one minute, with deep time, things move very slowly, you know."

"Oh yes, I can!  I'm the SSG Prefect and I move faster, I issue your digging permits on government land, time is money for you guys, that's why."

Alack broke a grin. "Gentlemen, your sea monster legend, the Macara, has something to do with our monster?"

"Yes, Colonel. According to our research…" both men nodded at another in respect, "the Macara really did exist. It is a direct descendant of Petio-Balarous. Trapped in deep water lakes it gave rise to the first colonists dragon and sea monster stories. Also, we've found it's fossils in the local mines and after much study determined it is a unique creature. It was once a land animal with paws that went back into the sea. Fossil evidence shows it was warm-blooded and had lungs, not gills, to breathe. Its fins had the bone and cartilage of a paw with five flexible digits."

"I thought all life here on E. Palis III came from the sea."

"It did Prefect," answered Argan. "But as geology changed, one species went back into the ocean to survive."

"We think Petio-Balarous originally was a Kugar-Ry (raccoon). They don't have saliva glands and must wet their foods so they can eat them. Fossil evidence shows a special organ to store items in, like the desert dromedary, the Flat-a-Hump (camel) with a bladder to store water for long periods. Petio-Balarous's fossils had such an organ filled with fragments of bone, rocks, and scales, separating the nutrients from the garbage."

"Certain rocks we've found by the fossil sites are made up of petrified pieces of the same, they're called Bitrolits. We only find them where the Petio-Balarous is found. Am I correct in saying that, Tellor?"

"Very much so, Argan." He held out a data disk as Alack took it.

"Anything else we should know?"

"Oh yes, one other thing, Prefect. We think it hibernates and is nocturnal. But don't hold us to that, it's only conjecture based upon related extinct species."

After the two are escorted from the crime scene, Gallopus stared at Alack. "Ya'know Colonel, you can be a real spike in my Scutum or a freaking Mentate with an attitude. Either way, I still admire you."

"I like the sound of all three."

It is the loud siren and breaking thrusters of three Deluxe Zos crammed with government agents that caught their attention. As the vehicles landed not far from them, Gallopus swore, spitting at the ground. "Damn, all Kranos's beasts! You've jinxed my crime scene, Colonel. They always come in threes..." Alack was about to say something but is cut off. "How'd he knows?"

"Is that who I think it is, Prefect?"

"Yes, the Royal Privy Counsel of Validor."

"You mean the provincial Prosecutor under your Curlator?"

"The same Colonel, after his promotion."

The bad memories burst back as Alack eyed the man in ever sickening waves. This is the agent who lied to Alack and made him fail in a full investigation, overlooking evidence that could have saved lives five years ago. The Irritant is still around and even more powerful. Alack fought down his suppressed anger trying to remain professional.

A skinny set Fellow with a curved headpiece that draped down to the white Nehru uniform of the government, a face of white-washed pastels frowned at both men. "You two are under arrest for the deaths of Director Lusitan and his friends.  Any resistance to my men will use lethal and dangerous force to make you comply."

"Sounds serious," began Gallopus, starting to chuckle.  "So Blankan, you wanted to put on a show and impress me, you've done a good job at it.  I guess even a rat like you must leave his lair sooner or later."

"This is right from the King-Curlator himself!"  The agitated Fellow began puckering his cheeks and making stuttering sounds as he held up a fancy scroll.

"How did you get that?"  Gallopus grabbed it, broke the ribbon seal, and unfolded the silken paper.  "Ha!  You even spelled my name wrong!  I ain't reading this…" he crumpled it and pushed the mess back into the Man's trembling arms.  "Go tell your corporate lackeys that I can't be bullied, kicked, or threatened, and that document is a farce to intimidate, now take your goons and get the Kranos off my crime scene before my men beat the crap out of your men.  I remember what you did five years ago, I don't forget!"  Gallopus stood defiant with hands on hips.  "Well…I'm waiting!"

The Fellow began to stutter, slobber, and pace back and forth. Hesitating, then backing off, finally made a decision.  "This isn't the end of this!"  He took his men and left, their Zo's rising so fast it rained dust and debris all over.

"Sergeant," an Aide saluted.  "Get their ID's and issue a ticket for improper driving."  He turned to Alack, "I guess you want an explanation.  That person is also the legal Privy whip of the Curlator's Council, but he's a pawn of Sylak and Milston that Lusitan worked for. We've butt heads before and every time he's backed off.  If he presses the issue, I'll indict him for falsifying legal documents to suit his own private needs."

"I recall him…that mandate was false?"

"As false as the Gas Microbe Theory, Colonel."

"On ancient Seminia the Privy Counselor was a guy who followed the King around with a wet cloth and chamber pot. His main job was to wipe the King's posterior after going to the bathroom."

"Don't you mean a fregging royal dump? You're so trim and proper Colonel, it's infecting even me. Blankar is still licking bottoms as a silly witty saying is overdone."

"Revenge has no bounds?"

"Not bad, I like that one. Let's check the other crime scene."


After finishing his analysis of the second crime scene by the mine, the LiDAR scan of the area revealed nothing extraordinary. Any DNA or bio-remains of the past occupants failed to be detected. The SSG with the University equipment scanned the areas around by shaft four and several Sectals out, finding nothing but rusted beer cans and some decaying plastic dinner trays. Even the new crime scene had scant evidence except for faint traces of the creature's DNA. It is a simple comment from the Geologist who provided an answer. The Blue Stone mineral, which is in the Validor hills, seems to block and distort the LiDAR beams. This was discovered since such a scan was never done in this area. Not perturbed, Alack knows it will excrete the undigested items in its belly soon. He must be there with Gallopus's men to catch it and destroy it. It is the only time they have to catch it at it's weakest and kill it before it begins feeding again. Time is of the essence; the clock is now ticking.

Becoming restless over his dilemma, Alack decided to check out the local street scene. Leaving the Praetorium by the back way, he came out on a side street of Validor City, led to a seedy part of the mining town. Wearing black boots, black pants, utility belt snugly around his thin waistline, Alack's upper torso stretching the white fabric of his short sleeve polo shirt without rank on the collar, the whole affair gravitated towards a corner pub down the street. A smiling holographic female on a billboard beckoned travelers in, but some of the electronics had failed and only obscene parts of her body blinked and winked. The faded sign on a shingle is also broken, someone had put sheet metal over it and painted it in neon glow colors, 'The Last Hole'.

'Yes...definitely an improvement over the shanty town.'

Getting an adventurous desire to test the social waters entered and sat down at the bar. The stench of stale liquor, lung weed, vomit, and other odors of unwashed bodies came at him like a twisting storm. The wood and brick décor is stained with grease, cobwebs, and wall pictures. These are so dirty, like the windows, that only an oily brownish tint obscured everything. Small sandy dirt covered the creaking floorboards as tables and booths flanked the bar on the street side of the room. What were curtains are mere rages, along with some union mining banners, long since forgotten by the owners and cliental. A long-buried memory opened. Yes, the days of past youth and student delights at the 'Farmer's Den', southwest of Villa Hardin. A similar place he missed, the fun, the crazy antics, part of his growing cycle.

To Alack's surprise a very well stocked cooler unit with shelves of alcoholic brews he recognized proudly occupied places behind the bar.  He recalled the time when him and three local farm boys decided to sample each.  The mess they made on the floor proved to them all he was as human as the rest.  A number of ancient machines, the forerunner of the Barbot, squatted on the back counter, gathering dust and rust.  Several large mirrors, on a slant, made the whole room visible from every angle the bartender needed.

"What's your pleasure?"  Asked a grizzly ugly Fellow in a soiled apron affair covering most of his rotund body.

"I see you have Unapiterian Brewmist…what year is it?"

"When Civeron, bless his whole torso, came to power, 2041."

"I'll take a glass of that, Sir."  Alack almost said 'wow', but stifled it.

"You look pretty fit under there, with the miners?"

"I'm part of the Prefect's investigator team, Sir."

"You ask me, they died the same five years ago.  The beast has returned."  He poured a large glass of Brewmist and a shot of the red liquor that goes with the other half of the square fancy embossed bottle.

"You think it's a creature of sorts?"  Alack tried to recall how much you mix with the glass, a few drops at a time or just dump it all in.  Not wanting to be amateurish, poured the full shot into the glass and gently swished it before sipping.

The Bartender smiled, knowing this guy has been around.  "It came from the bottom of shaft four, the guys dug too deep for those blue stones, unhatched a chamber of horrors, now it comes back to kill us all."

"You're scaring the handsome stranger Druf."  Two girls dropped their dainty asses on the stools on either side of Alack.  One is elderly with too much makeup and the other very young with no makeup. Both are overly friendly, almost drooling as they studied Alack the way he does over a steak dinner. "All that fuss over something that happened five years ago has nothing to do with what's happening right now."

"You think these are two different crimes?"

"Oh yes, yes…"

"The first one wiped out the whole town," added the younger Girl, "these are isolated incidents."

Alack went to sip his drink, and it was empty. "I've been working with the Prefect he thinks they're all the same." Alack made a second drink.

"Oh no, Sweets, two different things here," began the older lady, poking him in the bicep. "The Director killed the first monster with gas and microbe things from the University guys."

"And this one a new one, it came from the dumps outside of town." Spoke to the young girl with a smile.

Alack took his drink, and it was empty. "You say from the dumps?" He made a third drink. "They dump their garbage in a landfill rather than recycling it?"

"Oh yes, we both work for the Sanitation Office and it's cheaper to dump than recycle."

"Yes, very cheaper."

Alack went to taste his drink, and it is empty. Realizing he is in a setup to steal expensive drinks; he placed the empty glass down. Giving eye contact to each girl, he expressed himself in a firm accusation. "That's not only what's cheap around here. Stealing other people's drinks is wrong, Ladies. If I am to be hanged, let it be once. You both have jobs, what you earn should be enough for your nightly pleasures."

Both grabbed their purses, where the sucking device is located, and became defensive, using many swear words Alack never heard.

"Leave them girls alone!" came two men from a corner booth.

"They be good girls in this place."

"I heard what you said, and apologize!" Shouted a big Humanoid, and he needed a shave and a bath. By his expression, he did not understand the witticism but wanted to be brutal to impress the females.

Both girls, making further accusations, left their seats, taking Alack's bottle.

"I'm not apologizing Sir because I did nothing but speak the truth…"

"Well see about that!"

Alack saw it coming.

In one burst of speed, he pushed himself from the stool onto the Man's chest and had him on the floor in less than a second. Using a Jardellian finger technique, he put the Man out faster than he could respond. "The best of men fears nothing!"

The other Guy screamed, "You killed Frad! You bastard…I'll get you!" Whipping out a long screwdriver tool with a sharp blade at the end leaped down at Alack's shoulder.

Faster and quicker from his Special Service training, Alack swung his body aside. The deadly weapon splattered blood on the Man's forceps. Grabbed the man's wrist, applied a pressure point, forcing release of the deadly tool, and yanked him down to the floor next to his friend. Seeing total fear on the Guy's whitewashed face, used the moment to allow his ego to torment. "All four of you are in on this." The young man's green eyes are wide open. "On some planets they take an eye or a finger or a tooth for petty thievery, do you want to play that game with me?" A drool came from his startled mouth in a 'no' manner. "Your worst customers are your best teachers, so change your ways!"

Alack shot up. Deciding to make a Seminian example, took the metal stabbing tool and crumpled it like a pretzel. Tossing it on the bar left for the door.

"Hey!" Yelled the Bartender, "Who's paying for my Brewmist?"

"Those two…ladies are." And Alack left, returning to the Praetorium full of new ambition and purpose.

"I'm not sending an armed Trooper team down that shaft with scuba gear and underwater explosives to kill the creature!" shouted Gallopus.

"Macara," corrected Alack, he hates to be yelled at. "A great hunter will never quit."

"What the fregging Kranos you mean by that!?"

"We must examine all ways to kill it before it attacks again, Prefect."

"And as for the pump idea, flush it, Colonel. It would take years to pump out all that water going down to the bottom. We need a better idea."

"Why don't you people recycle?"

"What!  Now we're into recycling than killing this thing…the Macara?"

"The garbage dumps on the other side of town…that's where it will discharge its next load of indigestible matter."

"How do you know that, Colonel?"

"I went out with the University people in your Zo and scanned the dumps.  I found remains of people from five years ago, wallets, ID bags, some coins, personal jewelry with engraved names…plus lots of newer items from the crime scenes."

"You've made your point, Colonel."  Gallopus paused in his tirade.  He realized he could not fight this, but he took the opportunity and turned upon the Seminian.  "Okay, there's oil in the fryer, you're saying it'll go to the dump and do its thing, then we can kill it?"

"Yes, Prefect.  All my instincts point me to that site.  If you can gather your men, arm them, we can make a kill and stop your people from dying."

"Always the hunter, Colonel?  Since we don't know when I'll have my men place some biometric sensors to cover that area, we'll know when it's coming and be there ahead.  Think that'll fill the bill at the show?"

Yes, Sir, and I can go home."

"You don't like our cooking?"  Gallopus began to chuckle, seeing a light at the end of the terror tunnel.  "I'll get my men ready; they'll grumble over these night operations."

It was not long before the Macara monster was on the move. Sensor drones detected its mass carefully lumbering along the less traveled paths of the wastelands outside of Validor City.  With a curfew in place, an eerie silence descended upon the mining town.  The people shut up in their houses and knew something terrible was about to happen.  Even those who disdained law and order rules hid away, waiting for it to be all over and safe.

"I've got the bravest SSG men and those who received citations from the other cities on their bellies, Colonel.  All are armed with standard pistols…"

One of his Aide's wiggled himself between Alack and Prefect Gallopus.  "I brought the grenades from the SSG Armory, Sir.  But you're going to get a nasty-gram from the Service Captain at the Citadel."

"Why…by Kranos?"

"We stole them, by the time the paperwork is approved we would miss this opportunity…"

"Get those things out'a here, Corporal!  We have plenty of firepowers to melt that thing a dozen times over."

"Yes, Sir!"  And he wiggled his way out, pulling the munition box.

"I can't damn their enthusiasm, only control it, so many have felt this terror, Colonel, a nasty feeling that it'll never end and keep repeating itself."

"I know the emotion, Sir.  Several Affairs in the past seemed to be over but were only just getting started.  I don't like to be away from my home to long."

"You mean Seminia?"

"Amazia.  I have a place on a peaceful beach."

"Sounds like a great party local, Colonel."

The sixty men lay on their stomachs, at an angle sloping up to avoid hitting another in the face with photonics. The garbage dump stretched as a curved mound covered with a thin layer of gravel over two thousand Illos (roughly 84 feet). A fresh pile of trash spilled over the center, waiting for the city sanitation crew to spread it out with a dirt covering. Starlight twinkled down, shading the rocks with a bluish stark coldness during the summer evenings. An uncanny silence swept over the sixty men and several support personnel in a hastily built bunker to the side of the dump.

"It's on its way..." whispered an Aide studying the activated sensors on his Calcomp's screen. As something big and menacing approached, red dots blink along the sides of the image. "Coming in straight and steady...you'll see it between those rocks anytime now."

"Get ready men," ordered Gallopus from the bunker, "Squad Three, split and move to your right and left, give it a clear path in. Wait till it positions itself in the middle of the dump..." he paused glancing at Alack who drew his Higgons blaster, "are you ready, Seminian to bag your first monster?"

"Thrilled is more like it...the bravest men fear nothing...I'm moving in closer."

"Hear that men," said Gallopus in his collar mike, "the bravest men fear nothing... right from the heart of a Knight of the Sun...if this thing doesn't eat him first."

A light round of chuckling wisped passed on the refreshing breeze.

"You can't do this!" Came three men from the darkness behind the piled rocks serving as a command bunker, "I order you to cease and stop!" The funny Fellow in the overlapping curved hat and fancy Nehru government gown stepped out into the center of the dump site so all could see. "There is no monster!" He shouted.

"GET OUT OF THE LINE OF FIRE!" Screamed Gallopus leaping up, "It's coming your way, stupid!"

"One of your people killed Director Lusitan and his people, I have the evidence!"

"Blankar! Get your people out of there…!"

There is quivering darkness. Something massive, oily, and glistening pounced. What resembled a wiggling pod of squirming, yellow fanged fingers seized both of the government men. A soft gulping and the mass of a bobbing shrieking claw smacked Blankar aside. He died immediately from a crushed skull. A sickly rotting odor of blackish slime and fetish flesh wallowed in a slumping body at the center of the dump.

"THE LIGHTS AND FIRE!"

A dozen high-intensity spotlights exploded in a tidal wave of glaring brilliance.

What they saw took a moment of shock inhaling the horror.

Great and bulbous, with millions of tiny squirming creatures in a lattice of oily webs, quivered in a terror of jolting spasms as it reacted to the incandescence. A terrifying black ribbed maw of syrupy thumbs and pods with eyes shuck a bellowing burst of pain. Crustaceans along with the lumbering, folding greenish-black bodies seemed to embed themselves into the skin in a mad frenzy, avoiding the light. Massive and worm-shaped, it seemed to fall into itself as dozens of pinpricks of blazing photonics struck. It rolled, arched, and flattened, avoiding the annoying bursts of energy. With a squeezing rush of quivering blubber like tentacles, it lashed out, grabbing a Service Guard. Within seconds, the screaming man vanished beyond life's pleasures.

"My ray power isn't working!" gasped Gallopus, "try and get closer!"

Another SSG Man has swept aside as the whalish pulsating mass takes in another tidbit. This time a great seething yellowish claw struck out from a hidden orifice and grabbed another man. Others seeing this tried to dismember it with precision shots, but the blood sucking terror vanished within, the layers of protecting blubber hiding it. Again, it struck out, but from a different part of the massive bulk. A guard next to Alack is scooped up, legs and arms flailing high, and a deathly scream is sent down into its cavernous maw. The menacing claw moved within the gyrating membranes, popping out at the precise moment to feed.

"There's no defense!" Alack, jumped, leaping and rolling, placing bolt after lethal bolt into its hind quarters, realized they needed high photonics to even hurt this thing. Whatever the Petio-Balarous was, this giant slug of an ancient seaworm has evolved into something far more dangerous. Realizing he needed to act before other SSG Men were slashed away, he saw the box of grenades. Getting an idea, broke the wooden top with his fist and grabbed a dozen of the palm-sized balls and the control pad. Finding Blankar's dead body filled his pockets and clothes. Activating the mass detonator for five minutes seized the body and ran at the swinging gaping mouth. In one quick thrust tossed the body in and jumped head first over the edge of the dump pile.

A tasty morsel of human flesh vanished in one quick gulp.

In one titanic blast, the Macara creature filled the whole area with a mushroom of sticky green goo and thousands of indigestible shards. Up went the black cavernous blanket mass, separating into myriads of wobbling bits. It rained down for a good minute, a shower of slime and slurpy, wet pieces, stinging in an acid-bile wail of death. A few lights exploded as the cold gummy shards struck the hot lamps. When it cleared a motionless lump of material laid in the dump, nothing squirmed or quivered, only an uncanny silence swirled away until one of the SSG Men swore he is covered in filth.

They are all dressed in oily grease and stinking grime.

As the survivors struggled to stand, the SSG Men and Gallopus stepped circling the dead mass in the middle. Alack pushed his way upfront, at first unrecognizable, he received the full tsunami of gooey guts. The Prefect saw him and began to chuckle. Alack always seemed trim and proper, now this sight is quite refreshing. "By Kranos…what a wonderful smell you've discovered. Well, Colonel, I guess my men got the creature."

Realizing he is repulsive, avoided the humor, not allowing Gallopus to have the final say. "No, Sir, it wasn't your men, it was Blankar who killed the beast." The shocked expression only added to the overall mystery. "I'll explain later. Let's set fire to it's remains just to be sure. Everything in life is a trade-off."


THE END

# ABOUT THE AUTHOR

Ernest Velon lives in northern New Jersey, in the town of Hackettstown, USA. A confirmed bachelor, he is an amateur expert on Roman History and dabbles in archeology. His other interests are astronomy, geology, and the sciences. Ernest Velon's favorite sport is men's gymnastics, and he enjoys watching classic films and old Kung Fu movies. Inspired by the great writers of science fiction, The Man from Hardin and the Troyuan Chronicle book series features the exploits of Alack Troyus solving baffling crimes amongst the stars. A fan of Sherlock Holmes and the 'X Files', he has weaved a stunning Universe of intrigue and mystery in which his character thrives in. Ernest Velon also has the Thracian Bound, Thracian Unbound and Thracian Abroad cartoon series on the internet. These can be seen on Roku, VOD channel or Vimeo.com. For all of his scattered work and literary projects, go to his website at 'http://www.ernestvelon.com'.